THE TAKING OF MONTE CARRILLO

"What's the target?" The young Commando glanced enquiringly at Action Man lying under the shelter of a crumbled stone wall. "What do I aim at?"

"The house! The side of the house!" Action Man was busy pushing a new magazine into his Sten-gun. "I want a hole in the side of that house." He was feeling irritable and his voice was sharp with annoyance. "Just bang a shell through the side so's we can get in without going round to the front door and knocking!"

The Allied bridge-head had been under devastating attack. When Action Man and G.I. Joe learnt the secret of Monte Carrillo they knew it had to be taken — and destroyed.

3 cde

THE TAKING
OF MONTE CARRILLO

MIKE BROGAN

CORGI CAROUSEL BOOKS LTD
A DIVISION OF TRANSWORLD PUBLISHERS LTD

THE TAKING OF MONTE CARRILLO
A CORGI CAROUSEL BOOK 0 552 52075 6

Originally published in Great Britain by
Aidan Ellis Publishing Ltd.

PRINTING HISTORY
Aidan Ellis edition published 1977
Corgi Carousel edition published 1977

Carousel Books are published by
Transworld Publishers Ltd.,
Century House, 61–63 Uxbridge Road,
Ealing, London W5 5SA
Made and printed in Great Britain by
Cox & Wyman Ltd., London, Reading and Fakenham

CONTENTS

THE TAKING
OF MONTE CARRILLO

CHAPTER ONE

FAILURE!

"What's the target?" The young Commando glanced enquiringly at Action Man lying under the shelter of a crumbled stone wall. "What do I aim at?"

"The house! The side of the house!" Action Man was busy pushing a new magazine into his Sten-gun. "I want a hole in the side of that house." He was feeling irritable and his voice was sharp annoyance. "Just bang a shell through the side so's we can get in without going round to the front door and knocking!"

The house Action Man was talking about was the first one in a line of cottages that made up the village of Tavati. The village, no more than half a mile wide, consisted of a single main street, and the cobbled surface shimmered and shifted in a heat haze.

It was hot. The sun blazed down out of the blue Italian sky roasting everything below; scorching the fields and scrub; turning the soil into powdery dust and parching the throats of the British and American soldiers as they moved inland from the bridgehead they'd established on the coast at dawn.

And all the time the invaders had been under heavy shell-fire. Barely a second passed without the crashing blast of an explosion and an erupting fountain of earth occurring somewhere among the advancing lines.

The young Commando aimed his American Bazooka at the house and squeezed the trigger. The blow-back of flame burst from the rear of the Bazooka over his shoulder and the side of the house shuddered and cracked as the shell struck home.

"Give it another. I want a hole in there." A shell screamed overhead and exploded not far behind them. Debris showered down, bouncing off their steel helmets as they hunched.

Again the Bazooka spouted flame from its rear end and again a shell hit the side wall. This time a cloud of dust and smoke blossomed abruptly, and when it subsided they could see a sizeable hole.

Action Man nodded his head grimly. "Okay, let's go."

They rose to their feet and began to run, crouched over. A shell burst ahead of them and they threw themselves flat but before the torn earth had finished falling, they were on their feet again and running.

Action Man reached the house first. The hole they'd blown in the wall gaped invitingly. Action Man slid to a halt beneath it. He'd

10

already pulled the pin from the grenade he held and he loosened his grip letting the handle fly away; he counted off five of the seven seconds of the fuse and then tossed the grenade through the hole.

It exploded with a muffled roar inside the house and Action Man leapt through the hole. Dust from the explosion swirled inside, bits and pieces of plaster were still falling from the shattered ceiling. Action Man stood with legs braced and fired a long burst from his Sten-gun, raking the room from end to end. Then he raised the gun muzzle and fired another burst into the ceiling, swinging the arc of fire.

The young Commando was waiting outside beneath the hole his Bazooka had made, lying in the rubble. Action Man grinned down at him: "Okay, you can come in. We're all alone."

The Italian civilians who had once occupied the house had long since departed taking with them most of the furniture. From the window, looking down the street, Action Man guessed all the other houses in the village were abandoned, too. There was no sign of life.

"What do we do now?" Action Man's companion had propped up his Bazooka by the window-ledge and was carefully placing a container of half a dozen shells beside it. From the window his Bazooka could command the length of the street. He took off his helmet and mopped his brow, but his eyes never once left the quiet street.

"Wait for the others to get here," said Action Man. "They shouldn't be long, we weren't more than half a mile ahead of 'em." He took another Sten magazine from his ammunition pouch and reloaded. He'd fired off a whole magazine of thirty-two rounds in his one-man assault on the empty house.

The shelling outside had not let up for one moment and Action Man crouched by the hole in the wall and watched. Flashes of flame and fountains of earth rose high wherever he looked and the whining of the shells passing overhead was continuous.

"Big barrage," he said laconically.

"Reckon it's the Germans? Or the Italians?"

"Germans. Most of the Italian troops are further south." Action Man stood up and stretched himself. He was six foot tall, broad-shouldered, muscular and in the peak of condition. But he and his companions had been fighting since the dawn landing, and the searing power of the sun was taking its toll. Even in the shelter of the house the air was like the inside of an oven.

From his battle-pack, which he'd dropped to the floor, he took two small tins of soup and tossed one to the man at the window. He knocked two holes in the top of the tin with the point of his bayonet. "Let's have a stand-easy while we can. We're going to have a visit from Jerry soon. He'll be creeping down that road out there."

"What makes you think that? Looks empty enough now."

"The shelling! Not a round has landed on these houses yet. It's my bet the far end of the village is full of Nazis waiting to move in and take care of anyone who gets through their barrage." Action Man winked. "So keep your eyes open, Pete."

It was ten minutes later when Action Man, watching from the hole in the wall saw two figures emerge from a curtain of earth flung up by the shellfire. They came forward at a stumbling run, the stockier of the two men carried a portable radio-receiver strapped to his back. Action Man waved and they changed direction slightly, turning towards him.

"Welcome!" Action Man waved the tin of soup which he still held in his hand. "You're just in time for grub." He assisted the two men as they scrambled in through the hole and stood panting from their exertions. The man with the radio set was a British Commando, the other wore American uniform.

"Well, stone me!" exclaimed Action Man, grinning broadly and holding out his hand. "G.I. Joe! Nice to see you, buddy!"

The American took the proferred hand and slapped Action Man on the arm with enough force to make the big Britisher wince. "No wonder they call you Action Man . . . you sure get to places where the action is. How it's going, then?" He gave a quick glance around the shattered room. "This place safe?"

A shell, falling closer than any of the previous ones, shook the house so that part of the ceiling descended upon them in a shower of thick dust.

"It was until you got here." Action Man jerked his head towards the shattered wall. "Where's the rest of the boys? Time they got here, too, isn't it?"

G.I. Joe frowned. "Things are not so good. We sure took a battering getting here. Those guns were zeroed-in on us all the way. Seemed almost as though Jerry could see us and pick us off as he liked." He turned from Action Man and slipped off his ammunition pouches and pack. "I'm telling you now, there ain't many going to get this far."

The youngster at the window turned, startled. "But there were one hundred and twenty of us. They can't all . . ."

"That's one heck of an artillery barrage," broke in G.I. Joe. "Every time I took a look round I saw guys dropping like flies. Oh, sure, there'll be some of 'em who got through." He took a deep breath. "But not many. Don't count on many of 'em."

"There'll be reinforcements, though? There'll be others behind?"

From his pack, the American took several bars of chocolate and tossed one to each of the others. "Should go down well with the soup.

Eat up, it may be your last meal!"

The man who had arrived with G.I. Joe had been quietly setting up his radio-set by the hole in the wall. The extended aerial stuck out through the hole and he'd placed earphones and hand-mike neatly on top of the set ready for use. He peeled the paper from his chocolate bar and took a bite.

"So you two know each other?" He gestured with the chocolate bar from G.I. Joe to Action Man.

"We've done a bit of fighting together. Been in a few tight places together," said Action Man. He grinned at the American. G.I. Joe was similar in build to the British Commando, tough, rugged, steely-eyed and square-jawed. "Not a bad bloke to have around when there's trouble."

"For a Britisher," returned G.I. Joe, slowly, chewing rhythmically, "Action Man ain't so bad in a scrap." He moved his shoulders like a boxer in the ring. "You know . . . he can handle himself. Yeah, he's a buddy o' mine all right!"

"Movement across the street!" snapped out the man at the window suddenly. He pulled the Bazooka against his shoulder and squinted down the sight. "Over there. Getting into that third house from the back. Seven of 'em . . . eight . . . ten. Ten of 'em!"

G.I. Joe and Action Man slid across to the window. Action Man drew back the cocking-

handle of his Sten and the American did the same with his carbine.

The Bazooka-man relaxed. "It's okay, they're our blokes. They were in the shadow at first, didn't get a clear view."

"British or American?"

"Mostly British but a couple were Yanks. An' two were wounded, they were being helped along."

"Some more coming." This time it was the radio-operator by the hole in the wall. "Must be a couple o' dozen. Our lads all right."

"Two tanks, too." Action Man peered over the radio-man's shoulder. The newcomers were moving forward slowly but deliberately pressing on through the heavy shellfire. Now and again the men dropped and lay flat but they rose again and kept coming.

The tanks got to within two hundred yards of the village when shells hit both of them simultaneously. Both blew up with a tremendous roar and flash of fire. Black smoke rose high in the air from the shattered hulks.

"Both of 'em, crews an' all!" whispered G.I. Joe. "Never had a chance!"

The men moving along with the tanks had been obliterated in the huge fountain of earth that had been flung up, but now as it subsided, they could see four figures still moving forward. Moving faster now, trying to reach the cover of the houses.

G.I. Joe and Action Man watched in helpless

silence until the four men vanished from sight behind a house on the far side of the street.

"Two dozen men and — and two tanks . . . and only four of 'em made it," muttered the American. "Guess that's pretty tough."

"Did you see the four?" called Action Man. "Did you see them come round your side?"

The youngster with the Bazooka nodded. "Yeah. Four of 'em. They got into the house where the others went."

There was a long silence in the room. Overhead the shells continued to whine and snarl and the thump of each explosion shook the floor.

"I'll try to raise the beach-head and find out what's going on back there," said the radio-operator at last. He switched on the set and a muted howl of static filled the room. "Let's hope someone back there's listening out for us."

"What's your name, chum?" asked Action Man. "Might as well all introduce ourselves. We could be here together for some time."

"I'm Harry Parsons. D Company. Come from Devon when I'm at home."

"Bazooka-boy's Pete Thomson. A. Company with me. Londoner." Action Man gestured at the radio-set. "When you do get through, tell 'em where we are, village called Tavati. An' tell 'em there's just eighteen of us made it here and if Jerry makes a counter-attack, we're going to need ammunition. What we've got won't last long."

Harry Parsons nodded and slipped the earphones over his head, bending intently over the dials of the set. "Eagle One calling Eagle Base. Eagle One calling Eagle Base. Come in, Eagle Base. Over."

He repeated the call-signs over and over again without a reply and Action Man turned back to the window.

"Anything happening out here? Any movement?"

Pete Thomson looked puzzled. He was peering intently out into the street. "I'm not sure. I thought I saw something just now, right at the end of the street. But the shadows between the houses are so dark, it's difficult to be certain!"

"Saw what?" asked Action Man sharply. "What did you think you saw?"

"Just a movement. In the shadow. It could have been a man . . . up there about ten houses along on the far side. That one there." He leaned forward from the window to point and as he did so a burst of automatic gunfire shattered the wooden window frame behind him sending slivers of wood slicing into the air.

Pete Thomson dropped back, fell to his knees and toppled sideways. An ugly red stain began to seep from beneath his body.

For a split second Action Man stood frozen; then he snatched up his Sten-gun. Even as part of his consciousness had watched Pete Thomson slump to the ground, he had located a movement on the roof of one of the houses opposite. A man, a German soldier, crouched half hidden behind the chimney pot. There was a flash of fire as the German fired again and bullets smashed in through the window and shattered the plaster on the far side of the room.

At the same instant, Action Man opened fire. The Sten jumped in his hand. Brickwork on the chimney spurted into flying chips as the Sten-gun bullets searched for a target.

G.I. Joe was at Action Man's shoulder, his carbine cocked and ready. "Did you get him, buddy?"

Action Man shook his head slightly, keeping well to one side of the window, eyes glued to the roof opposite. Then, a machine-pistol fell on to the slates of the roof and slid down, falling over the edge and hitting the road with a clatter. Seconds later the sniper came into view. He took a tottering step out from behind the chimney and then fell backwards; for a moment his body rested over the ridge of the roof and then very slowly slid down the far side. The last glimpse they had was of the soles of the man's boots; then they too vanished.

"You got him!" grunted G.I. Joe.

They knelt beside Pete Thomson but there was nothing they could do for him. The sniper had swapped his own life for that of the young Commando.

"It'll put our chaps across the road on the

alert, anyway," said Action Man grimly.
"They'll know we're here . . . and they'll know
we've got Jerries in the village. We'd better
check our ammo. We've got a fight on our
hands."

"I'll get upstairs, to a back window," said
G.I. Joe. "Don't want 'em creeping up on us
from behind." He moved to the door that led
to the stairs and paused, glancing back. A
grim smile flickered across his lips. "Looks like
you and me are in business again, old buddy-
boy."

Action Man settled himself at the window
and waited, eyes fixed upon the sunlight and
shadow at the far end of the street. That's
where the assault would come from . . . and it
would come soon.

Harry Parsons gave up calling Eagle Base.
There had been no answer to his repeated
requests. He checked his Sten-gun to make
sure he had a full magazine.

"Try 'em again in ten minutes, Harry," said
Action Man softly. From the corner of his eye
he saw the man from Devon nod his head.

He's not easily scared, thought Action Man.
Good man to have around in a tight fix. Two
good men, he amended, thinking of G.I. Joe
keeping watch upstairs.

Minutes ticked slowly by and nothing
happened. Nothing moved. The shell fire was
still going on but it seemed to be further away.
The shuddering shake of the floorboards from

the bursting shells had diminished considerably.

G.I. Joe appeared in the doorway behind like a shadow. He whispered. "There's a Kraut creeping round the back of the house. He'll come by that hole in the wall in a couple o' minutes. He's alone."

Action Man made to move from the window but Harry Parsons had already flattened himself beside the shattered wall. He put out one hand with thumb held up.

A stone was dislodged outside. Then a shadow fell through the broken wall. Harry Parsons knelt down slowly, Sten-gun held ready, pointing.

The shadow moved and through the jagged opening came the barrel of a German MP40, a machine-pistol. Before the trigger could be squeezed, Harry Parsons leaned forward and grabbed the barrel, heaving it forward.

Instinctively the German held on to his weapon and he came tumbling in through the hole in the wall and finished sprawling inside the room on his hands and knees. Harry Parsons held the machine-pistol by its barrel.

The German was fat and middle-aged and wore the tabs of a private soldier. He remained on hands and knees, an expression of terror on his face. He was looking into the barrels of two Sten-guns and a carbine.

"Up, on your feet, chum," grated G.I. Joe. He swung the barrel of his carbine, leaving no room for doubt what he wanted the German to do.

And the man obeyed. Without further command he stood up and put his hands behind his head, backing off against the inner wall.

"We got a prisoner," grinned the American. He ran his hands over the man and removed two stick grenades from his belt. He also took the man's water bottle and tossed it to Harry. "Could be we'll need that."

Action Man resumed his position watching from the window. To Harry Parsons he said: "Try to raise the beach-head again. Tell 'em what's happening here." To G.I. Joe he added: "What are we going to do with this bloke? A prisoner is something we could do without!"

"We could shoot him," grinned G.I. Joe. "Can't think of anything else."

"NO!"

They stared at their prisoner in astonishment.

"Please, no. You cannot shoot me." The German still stood with his hands behind his head but his face had turned very pale. "Let me go, I will see you get good treatment. You will be forced to surrender soon. Your position here is hopeless."

"Hey, he speaks American," said G.I. Joe admiringly. "Now ain't that something."

"What do you mean, our position is hopeless?" put in Action Man. "What makes you say that?"

The German licked his lips nervously. "It is true. Your beach-head is finished. You will get no help. Our artillery has inflicted tremendous losses."

"He's just shooting off his mouth. How does he know?" G.I. Joe winked behind the German's back at Action Man and worked the bolt of his carbine. "Lemme shoot him. Get rid of him. He's just a pain in the neck to us."

"No. No. I'm telling you the truth." The German was becoming desperate, fully believing G.I. Joe intended to shoot him. "We have a defence system for this area. No one can move in the Plain of Carrillo without our observation system being able to pinpoint him. You will find out . . . already we have knocked out your tanks. Every tank that was landed has been destroyed. Your ships in the bay have suffered, too. Two destroyers have been sunk, many landing craft."

"How do you manage to pinpoint the targets so well? Tell me how and I might believe what you're saying?"

"We call it The Hill. It's real name is Monte Carrillo. You can see it from here, a huge hill, a mountain that stands in the centre of the plain. There is a castle on top, an old Italian castle, but inside the mountain we have built a communications system. Every single part of the Plain of Carrillo can be observed from The Hill. Our gunners are in communication with the men in The Hill . . . we can drop a shell on a single man if we wish . . . from ten miles away."

The German stopped talking. Action Man and G.I. Joe looked at each other in silence.

"He could be right," said Action Man.

"It would as sure as eggs explain how we came to take such a bashing from their guns," nodded G.I. Joe. He gave a low whistle. "If he is right . . . this Hill . . . this Monte Carrillo needs to be taken out of the game."

Harry Parsons looked up, his hands pressing his earphones against his head. "Hold on a minute . . . I'm getting something."

Then, distorted by heavy static, they heard a voice.

"Eagle Base calling Eagle One. Hear you loud and clear. Come in, over."

"It's them!" Harry Parsons grinned at them and switched the set to 'transmit'.

Briefly he told Eagle Base what had happened and where they were.

"Eagle Base calling Eagle One. Your message received and understood. Stand by for further orders. Over and out."

"How long will that be?" asked Action Man

Harry Parsons shrugged. "No telling. Could be ten minutes, could be a couple of hours." He smiled. "At least they know we're alive and kicking."

"And they're alive and kicking too." G.I. Joe looked grimly at their prisoner. "You've been lying buddy-boy. Our bridge-head is still in business."

"Lock him up. Find a cupboard back there somewhere and lock him up," snapped Action Man. He glared at the German. "You make one move, mate . . . and I'll let him loose on you," he stabbed a finger at G.I. Joe, "and you know what he'd like to do!"

G.I. Joe was still in a back room, securing their prisoner, when rapid firing broke out from the house across the street where the other group of Allied soldiers were taking shelter.

A German tank was nosing cautiously down the street and running behind it, crouching for shelter were a dozen German infantrymen.

The tank's turret began to revolve, its long barrel searching for the house from which the firing was coming.

"Tiger tank!" snapped Action Man. "If they get that eighty-eight gun going, they'll blow that house to pieces and our lads with it."

He loaded the Bazooka, resting the long barrel on the window-sill, sighting it on the Tiger tank's tracks. "Come a bit nearer, just a few yards. Come on, Jerry . . . nearer . . ."

And the tank continued to move forward. G.I. Joe was back beside Action Man, his carbine ready. "Reckon you can hit it?"

"I can hit it. Knock its tracks off. But I'm not sure whether or not I can put the gun out of action." The big Britisher squinted along the sights. "We need a bit of luck!"

The recoil of the Bazooka nearly knocked Action Man flat on his back. The recoil flame from the rear end seared across the room and left a blackened and scorched scar on the wall behind.

The Bazooka shell hit the Tiger tank squarely in the forward end of its tracks and half turned the machine around. The turret gun which had just come to bear upon its target, continued to turn slowly. It made a complete circle and began going round again . . . and again.

"You've done something to the turret! You've fouled up the electrics or something!" G.I. Joe clapped his hand on Action Man's back, whooping in delight. "Boy, o-boy. That's some shooting!"

"I said we needed a bit of luck!"

The tank began to move backwards, its driver hoping to reverse away down the street where some sort of repairs could be made in safety. But he hadn't reckoned with the damaged track.

As the tank moved backwards, so it began to turn on its one wrecked track. And as it turned, the German infantrymen were exposed.

G.I. Joe and Action Man opened up a devastating fire at the same moment as the men in the house opposite began firing. The Germans turned to run for shelter but before any of them reached safety, the fire of the Allied soldiers cut them down.

Within seconds the firing stopped. The street was littered with the bodies of the dead Germans. Only the tank was still moving. It completed a half circle and then its rear end rammed into the wall of a house, bringing half the brickwork toppling down around it. The turret had stopped revolving and now the hatch opened and a man appeared. He leaped down to the ground and made half a dozen paces before a single shot dropped him in his tracks. The rest of the crew remained inside, trapped.

G.I. Joe picked up the two stick grenades he'd taken from their prisoner. "I think we ought to return these to the Germans, don't you?"

"Don't take any risks," warned Action Man. "I need you alive!"

G.I. Joe tossed one of the stick grenades nonchalantly into the air and caught it by the handle as it came down. He winked. "Trust me, buddy-boy. Trust me!"

He had barely left the house when Eagle Base came through on the radio. Harry Parsons acknowledged and waited for orders.

The news was dismal.

"You are to return to the beach-head as soon as possible."

Action Man flapped an arm at Parsons. "Tell 'em about our prisoner; about that Monte Carrillo place."

Harry Parsons passed the message and Eagle

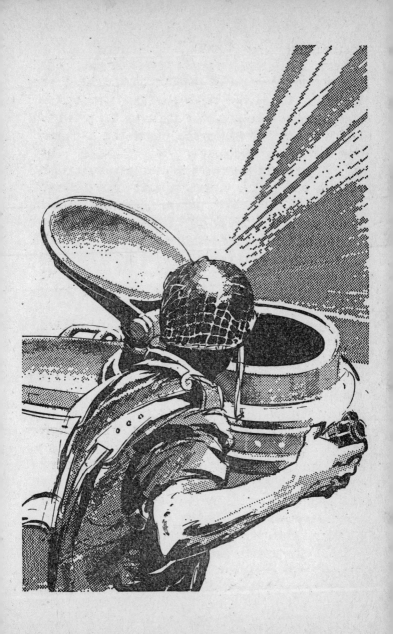

Base showed more than usual interest, asking him to repeat and clarify several times. Then he was told to stand by.

While Harry was talking to Eagle Base, G.I. Joe reached the disabled German tank, tossed the two grenades into the turret and slammed the hatch on them.

The noise of the two explosions was strangely muffled, like the sound of someone hitting a blanket with a cane. Wisps of smoke rose in thin streamers from the edges of the closed hatch and from the ventilator ports. The tank never moved again and the crew made no effort to escape.

"They won't escape," said G.I. Joe cheerfully. "The tank's had it and so have they!" He mounted the stairs to the look-out position he'd held before. "Jerry won't like it, you know," he cautioned. "I reckon we can expect a little more action soon!"

It was late in the afternoon when Eagle Base called again. Even through the static it was easy to recognise a different voice. This voice was incisive and commanding.

"Hallo, Eagle One. General Morecombe speaking. Get your senior officer to the set, will you?"

"Sorry, sir, no officers or N.C.O.s present. Action Man of the Commandos in charge." Harry Parsons glanced at Action Man and raised his eyebrows enquiringly as he spoke and Action Man nodded.

Harry Parsons vacated his position and Action Man donned the earphones and took the hand-mike, introducing himself to Eagle Base.

"This information you've had about Monte Carrillo, how much reliance do you put upon it?" General Morecombe sounded as cool and calm as though he were discussing a minor problem in the safety of a barracks.

"I think it's the truth, sir. Our prisoner was in fear of his life at the time, very, very frightened. He told us about Monte Carrillo to convince us that we weren't going to win."

"Our bombers have already plastered the place."

"The communications and observation area is located in the centre of the mountain. I don't think bombing would do much damage."

The General sounded thoughtful, talking almost to himself. "We've suspected something like this, of course." There was a long pause. And then: "Look here, Action Man, how many chaps have you got there with you? Any chance of you getting a closer look at Monte Carrillo. You're not far from it now, say ten kilometres."

"There's eighteen men here, sir, in two groups. At least two are wounded. We're pinned down at the moment but we could break out under cover of darkness."

"And you could get to Monte Carrillo and reconnoitre? I want to know just what goes on

31

there; how vulnerable the place is."

"We'll try, sir. We ought to be able to make a report by dawn."

"Hmm. 'Fraid I can't send you any help. We're pinned down here, too. We've got to knock out that damned Hill."

"If we reach Monte Carrillo, get real close, sir, we could try to sabotage it somehow."

The General sounded less than enthusiastic. "You'd have to get inside the place to do any lasting damage, Action Man. Hundred-to-one against, I'd say."

"If it's worth a go, we'll try, sir."

"If you could bring it off, Action Man, you'd save hundreds of lives. We can't break out of this bridge-head until The Hill is knocked out. The success of this operation depends upon that, make no mistake." Another long pause and then the General made up his mind. "Very well, you have your orders, Action Man. Locate, report upon, and destroy Monte Carrillo." And he added softly, "Good luck."

The static cut off abruptly and Action Man removed his headphones.

Harry Parsons stood rubbing his palms together. It was apparent he'd heard the conversation for he said: "Suicide mission, eh?"

"Could be," responded Action Man grimly. "But it may not be as crazy as it sounds. Eighteen, or sixteen of us will take a bit of stopping. We can get to Monte Carrillo by midnight . . . and if we can get inside . . . we could bring it off."

G.I. Joe shouted down from upstairs. He sounded excited. He also sounded puzzled. "Hey, Jerry's pulling out of the village. There's a tank and half a dozen trucks moving away. Moving fast, too . . . inland."

A clattering of hurrying feet down the stairs and the American appeared in the doorway. "Whaddya make of it, buddy-pal? They're making us a present of the village!"

"I don't like it. Why should they do that?" Harry Parsons was equally at loss and uneasy.

Five minutes later, they had their answer. A shell screamed overhead and dropped with a shuddering explosion not thirty metres from them. A second shell landed on a house across the road. Then the world seemed to become a crashing, shattering inferno of destruction. All three dropped flat, their ear-drums stunned by the thunderous noise.

"That's your answer," shouted Action Man. "They're not risking any more men or tanks against us. They're going to blow us to pieces. They're razing the village to the ground."

CHAPTER TWO

A LOAD OF TROUBLE!

The artillery assault on Tavati lasted thirty-seven minutes during which time over five hundred high-explosive shells fell upon the street and houses, reducing the entire area to a mound of rubble.

Action Man, G.I. Joe and Harry Parsons could do nothing but wait and hope for the barrage to stop. They crouched, huddled together underneath the staircase, partly protected by the chimney breast which rose close to the stairs above them.

One shell made a direct hit upon their house, bringing it down around them. Dust rose in choking clouds. Beams and masonry crashed around them, piling high in a confusion of debris. But miraculously the chimney remained intact and it was the stout brickwork rising above them that saved their lives.

Coughing and spluttering they crawled clear as the shelling ceased and silence reigned. Not complete silence; it was punctured by the crackle of flames and the intermittent fall of roof slates and bricks.

"The guys across the road. Let's help 'em."
Action Man stumbled from the ruin and stared
about incredulously. Battle-hardened though he
was, the devastated village shocked him. Not
one house could be recognised as such, scarcely
a wall was left standing and above the chaotic
scene rose a dense pall of dust and smoke.

G.I. Joe and Harry Parsons, stunned expres-
sions on their faces, joined the big Commando.
"Where do we start looking?" G.I. Joe gestured
uncertainly. "They were in the fourth
house . . . wherever that is."

On the far side of the street, one pile of
rubble was indistinguishable from another, the
shattered masonry merged into one long continuous pile.

"Let's start searching." Action Man glanced
up at the swirling smoke and dust-clouds. "No
one's going to see us under that lot . . . even if
they're looking."

No sooner had they commenced picking
among the debris than they realised it would be
a miracle if they found anyone alive.

*   *   *   *   *

Finally, they had to give up. They found
bodies but no survivors and although they con-
tinually called and listened with their ears close
to the wreckage, there was no answering sound.

"They've had it! All of 'em," muttered Harry

35

Parsons, shaking his head slowly. "We're wasting our time." The dust cloud was settling and it coated all three of them with a fine covering of white powder. And it was cooler. The searing sun was slipping to the horizon.

G.I. Joe turned to the house where they had sheltered, its cracked chimney stack rising like a rickety tower. He started towards it. "We've forgotten our prisoner. I locked him in that cupboard. Poor guy might still be alive. We can't leave him."

The prisoner was alive. The cupboard had fallen with the wall to which it had been fastened and rubble was piled high on top. The German must have felt as though he'd been lying in his coffin.

"Danke! Danke!" he kept repeating as they pulled him free. His face was badly bruised on one side and he trembled violently when he stood up. He let out a flood of German before the sight of the perplexed faces made him recall the language barrier.

He began to speak in English. "You save my life. I thank you. Thank you. If ever I can repay, I will, this I promise."

"You might get your chance sooner than you think," grunted Action Man. He gestured to the others. "Okay let's get moving. There aren't as many of us as we thought, but we'll still have a go at this Hill place. I reckon we owe it a few knocks."

"You're still going to try to get to Monte

Carrillo? With just the three of us?" Harry Parsons was aghast.

"Four of us," Action Man corrected. "We've got him." He jerked his thumb at the German soldier. "He can fetch and carry for us. If he tries to give us away . . . his luck will run out."

The German was listening intently and when Action Man asked if he understood, he nodded, but he didn't seem very happy.

G.I. Joe slapped the butt of his carbine and turned the muzzle at the Nazi. He showed his teeth in a ferocious grin. "I'll take care of him personally. Even if he *looks* like ratting on us, I'll put him down. You savvy, chum?"

The man nodded again, eyeing G.I. Joe warily. He now looked thoroughly miserable.

"Right, let's move up to the other end of the village. We'll wait there until it's dark and then make as fast a time as possible to The Hill." Action Man jerked his head at the German and the four men moved off, boots crunching on broken glass that littered the street.

The last house in the village had been far bigger than the others and of more solid construction. Action Man guessed it had been the Town Hall. It had been wrecked by the shelling but one centre wall remained and they picked their way across the sea of bricks and sat down with their backs to it.

The big British Commando squinted at the sun and estimated another hour to dusk. Harry Parsons still carried the radio set on his back

and Action Man told him to treat it with care.

"We may not get back ourselves, but we should get time to send a radio signal. Whatever we can tell 'em back at base about Monte Carrillo may well be vital."

"How much ammo do we have between us?" G.I. Joe was carefully cleaning the dust from the breech of his carbine, easing the bolt, making sure the mechanism was working smoothly. "I've got something like thirty rounds."

"Three magazines for my Sten," said Harry Parsons.

"I've got two." Action Man shook his head. "Not a lot. And no food or water." He thought of his pack buried in the house at the other end of the village. All their equipment apart from their weapons had been lost.

"Might be something here." Harry Parsons stood up and kicked at the bricks scattered in piles. "Ol' Jerry must have been using this place before he pulled out. He might have left some gear behind. I mean, they pulled out in a big hurry, didn't they?"

Confirmation of Parsons' guess came from the German prisoner. "This place was our store. Many ration packs were held here." The German was obviously feeling the pangs of thirst and hunger, too.

"Let's look around then." G.I. Joe rose to his feet and gestured to the German to do the same. "Look around chum but don't wander too far, okay?" He cradled his carbine significantly in one arm. "I'll have my eye on you."

The search looked like being fruitless, until pulling aside a huge beam, G.I. Joe revealed a flight of stone steps leading down. In falling across the steps the beam had sheltered them from the crashing masonry. At the bottom was a closed door.

"A cellar!" G.I. Joe moved down the steps whooping in delight. "There's gotta be some goodies stored in here. I got a feeling! There's gonna be a pile of German sausage a mile high inside."

He had his hand on the cellar door when Action Man's voice whipped out like a lash. "Hold it, Joe. Don't touch anything. Don't open that door."

"Why the heck not?"

"Booby traps!" Action Man's face was grim. "Jerry leaves 'em behind all the time. Let's open that door from a distance."

Action Man and G.I. Joe were wearing belts, Harry Parsons wore braces. The three items were joined together to form a makeshift rope and one end hooked over the door handle. Then, taking cover behind a hastily piled mound of bricks and stonework, they pulled. The door opened easily and noiselessly.

"A prize pack of idiots we must look," grinned G.I. Joe.

"I had a pal once who opened the door of a larder in a bombed-out house. He was looking for food. As he opened the door, he pulled the pins out of two grenades fixed inside," said Action Man grimly. "He never knew what hit him."

There was a moment of silence and then G.I. Joe said: "Yeah, guess you're right, buddy. But there ain't no booby-trap on that door, let's take a look inside."

G.I. Joe descended the steps and vanished inside the cellar. A moment later he looked out, an expression of astonishment on his face. "There's three guys in here!" he exclaimed. "Trussed up like chickens. A sergeant, a private and a civvy. All of 'em Britishers, I guess. At least, the two in uniform are."

The men in the cellar were released and led stumbling in the sudden light of day, out of the underground darkness.

Action Man regarded the new arrivals to his small force with approval. The sergeant and the private both bore the shoulder flashes of an infantry division. The N.C.O. was short and stocky with ginger hair and a face that looked as though it had seen many years of soldiering; a row of medal ribbons sewn on his battle-dress blouse confirmed this. Action Man guessed him to be a regular Army man in his late thirties.

The private was taller, barely an inch less in height than Action Man himself. He was about twenty-two, close-cropped dark hair and a stubble of black beard. His shoulders were as wide as a London bus. He was grinning and he spoke first.

"Thought we'd all had it in there, mate. When I heard the guns and all that stuff falling on top of us I said to myself, Victor, old mate, you've had your blooming chips. A nice long lingering death, buried alive."

Action Man moved in front of the sergeant. "How come you three were down there tied up, sergeant? How'd you get there?"

"Jerry took us prisoner two days ago." The sergeant's voice was hoarse and he licked his dry lips. "We could do with a drink. The dust inside that place when the shelling was going on was like a Sahara sand storm."

"You'll get a drink as soon as we find water, we're looking around for some now."

Harry Parsons who had been standing listening took the hint and moved away to continue the search among the rubble, pushing the German ahead of him.

The civilian, a middle-aged man in a suit of tweeds, pushed past the sergeant aggressively. His white shirt was grimed and his tie awry. He had a small moustache and held himself stiffly.

"Look here, whoever you are. I'd better introduce myself. Major Brinkley, Army Intelligence. I don't intend to stand here being questioned by you. I suggest you take me to your commanding officer. That's an order."

G.I. Joe said: "You don't look much like a Major to me, chum. More like the gardener."

The man in civilian clothes turned a bright

red and seemed about to explode.

"He's a Major all right, chum," put in the sergeant quickly. "He was in the plane with us."

"Plane? What plane?" Action Man decided to ignore the bristling Major for the moment and gave the sergeant his full attention. Major Brinkley had the appearance of being a load of trouble.

"We was in this plane. Took off from Sicily," said the sergeant. "A Dakota. We were flying to England. There was a storm and I reckon the pilot got a bit lost. We should have kept over the sea. But we didn't 'cos when it was dark a load of blooming ack-ack guns opened up on us. The plane got hit a couple of times and we had to come down. There was a crew of three up front and they all copped it when we crash-landed." He gestured at the other two "We were luckier, sitting in the fuselage, got out of it with just a few bruises.

"Jerry was on us immediately, of course. Took us prisoner and locked us up in that cellar. Nearly two days we been down there. Then they all went off and the shelling started . . . and then you showed up. We was pretty glad to see you, I can tell you."

Major Brinkley had become increasingly restive during this recital and he burst into speech again. Red-faced, angry.

"I've stood enough of this. As soon as I find someone responsible I shall have you put on a charge. Both of you." He glared wildly at Action Man and G.I. Joe in turn. "You may think being an American will save you from disciplinary action but I can assure you it won't."

"There's no officer here, sir," said Action Man patiently. "These men and myself are on a special mission. I'm leading them. We've had direct orders from General Morecombe."

"General Morecombe?" A lot of the bluster evaporated from Major Brinkley's manner. "Well, where is he? I'll speak to him."

"He's at the bridgehead, seven or eight kilometres back sir, and I should imagine there are now a lot of German soldiers between us and him."

"We — we're cut off?"

"That's about it," said Action Man cheerfully. "You might be out of the cellar . . . but you're not out of the wood, not by a long way."

Major Brinkley subsided completely, digesting the new information. The infantry sergeant spoke up again.

"There's something else you ought to know, chum," he told Action Man. "This bloke," he jerked his thumb at the crop-headed soldier next to him, "is my prisoner. I'd been detailed off to take him back to England in that plane for court-martial. We were hand-cuffed together only I took the cuffs off just before we crashed. Thought we might both have a better chance if we weren't tied together, like."

"We've got a right bunch here," put in G.I. Joe. "What's he done?"

"Murder!" said the sergeant. "Killed a corporal in Sicily."

"It wasn't no murder!" The soldier looked coldly at Action Man. "I did it in self-defence. Corporal Atkins attacked me. He asked for what he got."

"What's your name?"

"Blade. Victor Blade. Private Victor Blade."

"And you?"

"Sergeant Alan Jackson."

"He should never have taken the handcuffs off him." Major Brinkley's voice contained a note of apprehension. "A man like that. He's not safe."

"What's up, Major? Frightened I might sneak up behind you and shoot you in the back?" Blade grinned, showing a row of yellow, uneven teeth. It was a wolfish look. "How could I? I ain't got a gun!"

Major Brinkley opened his mouth to say something but was forestalled by the arrival of Harry Parsons and the German prisoner. They both carried half a dozen water bottles.

"Water in 'em, and it's good stuff," announced Harry. "They're Jerry water-bottles so I made Fritz give 'em all a taste, just to make sure. He's coming in handy after all."

The men who had been released from the cellar took the bottles eagerly and even the Major forgot his rancour in his desire to drink.

Action Man took G.I. Joe to one side, out of ear-shot. "You're right, Joe. We've got a right bunch with us now. An officer who looks as though he's never fought anything tougher than a pen on a desk, a murderer, and a Jerry. Sergeant Jackson looks as though he can handle himself, though. He'll be an asset."

G.I. Joe stared at Action Man in disbelief. "You can't mean it. You can't mean . . . we're going to take that lot with us . . . to Monte Carrillo? You must be joking, buddy. They're nothing but trouble. We'll either get ordered out of our minds by that maniac Major . . . or get our throats cut by the other guy, Blade. The German Army's enough to take on . . . without these guys!"

"We need 'em," declared Action Man. "Seven of us will do a lot better than four. I admit things might get a little dodgy but we've got to use 'em. They can fire a gun and that's all I ask of 'em."

"I wouldn't bet on that. Major Brinkley's never fired anything in his life. An armchair officer."

"He's not going to like taking orders from me, either!" Action Man winked at G.I. Joe. "But he's going to!"

When Action Man and G.I. Joe returned to the others they were offered a German ration pack by Harry Parsons. "Big box of 'em under the rubble near where we found the water bottles," he told them. He munched contentedly.

46

"Not bad for Jerry grub, either. Quite tasty."

The others had seated themselves to eat and drink and Action Man took the opportunity of delivering a speech while they were quiet.

Briefly he told them about Monte Carrillo and the communications post inside the mountain. They listened in silence, even Major Brinkley listened without interrupting.

Then Action Man said: "As soon as it's dark, which will be in less than quarter of an hour, we'll move forward. And we move as fast as we can. The sooner we get to The Hill, the more hours of darkness we'll have to check it out and maybe find a way of putting the place out of action.

"If we bump into the German Army on the way, we'll go round 'em. We don't want trouble before we get there. But, if we should be lucky enough to meet a patrol, a small one, say no more than ten men, we'll take 'em on. We'll knock 'em out as quickly and quietly as we can. The only purpose in doing this will be to acquire their weapons and ammunition, we're running short on those items ourselves. Got it?"

Major Brinkley rose to his feet. He had contained himself while Action Man had been speaking but now his anger bubbled over.

"Am I to assume that your intention is to remain in command even though I am the only officer here? If that is so, soldier, you're mistaken." He braced his shoulders and glanced around. "I am taking command of these men.

They will do what I say . . . and so will you.

"The first thing you should all know is this. The Monte Carrillo operation is off. It's sheer foolhardiness to attempt to make an attack on a German strongpoint with seven men. One of whom is a German prisoner." He gave a short bark of derision. "Absolute nonsense. And then we have a murderer! What sort of help do you think you'll get from him? He's more likely to cut and run when the going gets rough. No, General Morecombe, as I understand it, gave you your orders when he believed you to be a group of eighteen men. Now the situation is very different. We will not go forward. We will make our way back to the beach-head. This operation can be mounted some other time when it will stand a chance of success."

Action Man slowly and deliberately removed the magazine from his Sten-gun, studied it to make sure it was a full one and then banged it back into position. He held the weapon casually but the muzzle pointed at Major Brinkley.

"I'll say this just once!" His voice cut through the air like the honed edge of a razor. "We are all going to Monte Carrillo, starting from here in five minutes time. Any orders that are given will be obeyed instantly by all of you. And unless I say otherwise the orders come from me . . . and from me only." His eyes held Major Brinkley, glittering like slivers of ice. "You, sir, will do precisely what you're told to do by me, same as the rest of 'em." He glanced briefly at Sergeant Jackson. "That goes for you, too, sergeant. Understood?"

"Understood." Sergeant Jackson had summed up the situation and was not prepared to exert his own superiority of rank. "This was your show, Action Man, and as far as I'm concerned it stays your show. You're the boss."

"I do not intend to take orders . . ."

Major Brinkley's pompous speech died away abruptly as Action Man pulled back the cocking-handle on the Sten. "I am under orders from General Morecombe. Anyone . . . *anyone* who tries to stop me carrying out those orders will be shot."

The Major licked his lips which had gone suddenly dry. When he spoke his voice was a croak. "You'll hear more of this . . . afterwards." His tone became more vicious. "And I'll make you regret you were ever born."

"Anyone else got anything to say?"

Private Victor Blade moved until he stood in front of the muzzle of Action Man's gun. His smile was confident and twisted. "I ain't going on no suicide job, mate. An' you can't make me. I'm up to here," and he touched his head, "up to here in trouble already. But if I'm going to face death, mate . . . I'd rather face it in a British court with a British judge in charge and not in front of the German Army." He pushed another step forward so that his chest was touching the Sten muzzle. "You ain't going to shoot no-one, are you? Because you don't want

49

no noise what'd bring Jerry out here looking for you. I'm with the Major . . . I'm for heading back to the bridgehead."

G.I. Joe was standing beside Action Man and he caught the Sten-gun as the British Commando tossed it to him. In the same movement, Action Man raised his left boot and brought the outside of it scraping down on Blade's shin bone. His right-hand came round in a chopping motion and hit Blade just below the ear.

It was a blow that would have K.O'd most men. Blade went down on his knees but pulled himself together and as he rose his cold eyes were fixed upon Action Man in a gleam of hatred.

"You're gonna get what Corporal Atkins got," he hissed, and hurled himself forward arms out, reaching for Action Man in a bear-hug.

But Action Man wasn't there. He moved with the speed and power of a panther. This time his fist hit Blade in the mid-riff, doubling him over and then he brought his knee up into the man's face.

Blade dropped again, blood spurting from his nose. His hand groped for a brick and Action Man's boot stamped down on to his wrist and stayed there.

Action Man knelt beside his opponent and in his hand he held his Commando knife. He showed it to Blade. "I could use this on you and it wouldn't make any noise. Wouldn't bring any

Germans running. Now, where are we all going?"

Blade stared, mesmerised by the knife held within inches of his throat. Blood from his nose spread across his cheek.

"Where are we going?" repeated Action Man. "I'll give you five seconds to tell me!"

Blade's mouth worked. It opened and shut . . . and opened again. "Monte Carrillo," he mumbled. "We're going to Monte Carrillo."

Action Man rose to his feet, the knife vanished from view. He took the Sten-gun as G.I. Joe held it out to him. Dusk had fallen suddenly while the fight had been in progress. Looking across the shell-battered street he could scarcely make out the ruined houses there.

"Okay Sergeant Jackson, you take the lead. Destination, Monte Carrillo, some ten kilometres ahead and due West. The rest of you follow the sergeant, stay as far behind him as you can without losing sight of him. If you see or hear anything . . . go to ground and stay quiet."

Blade had climbed unsteadily to his feet, mopping his still bleeding nose.

"You walk at the back, just in front of me," ordered Action Man grimly. "If you do anything I don't like you will be a dead duck for sure."

They began to move out of the ruined village. Not the fighting unit Action Man would have liked, but all he could muster. He wondered what would happen when they went into action.

"Ain't gonna be no picnic, buddy-boy," whispered G.I. Joe falling into step beside the Commando. "But I gotta hand it to you for the way you dealt with Blade. That guy ain't no pushover in a punch-up but he didn't have a chance."

"If we do manage to capture some German weapons, Joe," Action Man replied softly. "Don't let Blade have one. He'd use it on me the first chance he got."

"He'd use it on all of us, I reckon," the American replied. "Cut us all down and hop off by himself. He's on a murder rap already, another half dozen victims won't make any difference."

"Is Harry Parsons looking after the Jerry prisoner?"

"Yeah, they're in the middle of the column with our friend the Major."

"Good. Stay here with Blade, Joe. I'm going up front with Jackson. We've got to move fast. I want to be at The Hill before midnight."

CHAPTER THREE

NIGHT FIGHTING !

The pace set by Action Man was blistering.
They walked on the grass at the side of the road
and relied upon Sergeant Jackson's keen eyes-
ight to warn them of danger. Now and again
Action Man relieved the sergeant at the head of
the tiny column, striding on ahead, eyes prob-
ing the enveloping darkness.

Barely an hour had passed when Major
Brinkley began to protest. "This is ridiculous,"
he snorted as Action Man called a halt to listen
to the officer's complaints. "If we do arrive at
this — this Hill place — none of us will be in
any condition to fight. We'll be exhausted." He
lifted a foot. "And look at this! I can't keep up
with you wearing these things. Civilian shoes.
They're falling to pieces already."

It was true. Major Brinkley's brown brogue
civilian shoes had split and the sole of one was
coming away from the upper.

But there was nothing Action Man could do.
His eyes met those of G. I. Joe and the American
shrugged and shook his head.

"You'll just have to keep walking . . . and keep up with the rest," Action Man told the Major. "And keep quiet."

The column continued on its way. At half-past ten Sergeant Jackson, who was leading, came back towards them running quickly and soundlessly on the grass verge.

"There's a farmhouse ahead. Lights on inside and a couple of vehicles in the yard. I think they are Panzer Mark Threes. I've come across 'em before out in the desert."

Action Man told the others to stay where they were and remain hidden, then he and the sergeant went forward.

The farmhouse showed up darkly like a silhouette against the sky. There were two buildings, the house itself and a big barn close behind. Both buildings showed bare ribs of roof rafters where tiles were missing. Close to the barn were the two tanks Jackson had noticed earlier.

"What's the crew of a Mark Three?" whispered Action Man.

Jackson held up a hand, spreading all five fingers.

An occasional light showed at the farmhouse windows where sacking which covered the broken panes, fitted badly. A low murmur of voices reached their ears.

"If there's just the tank crews in there, we could do for 'em," whispered Jackson. "Won't be more than ten men."

"Maybe only eight inside." Action Man inclined his head towards the dimly seen tanks. "There's two sentries over there." Action Man touched Jackson on the shoulder and gestured, jerking his thumb back over his shoulder. Silently they retreated.

"It's madness!" exclaimed Major Brinkley when Action Man explained his plan. "You said yourself there might be more than ten of them. How can we overcome them? There's only three of us with weapons."

"You'd be surprised what me and Action Man can do, mate," grinned G.I. Joe. "Believe me, we're experts!"

"Do not call me, 'mate'!" rasped the Major irritably. "I am an officer."

"You are a pain in the neck, too," rejoined G.I. Joe cheerfully. "I reckon we ought to give you this," and he hefted his carbine on one hand, "and send you in by yourself. I reckon an officer like you could deal with all those Nazis in no time."

Major Brinkley glared venomously at the American but decided not to reply and even in the darkness it could be seen his face had become noticeably less ruddy.

"You won't have to do anything, Major, at least, nothing that will bring you into contact with the enemy just yet," said Action Man crisply. "G.I. Joe and I will handle this. You will stay here and take charge of these two." He nodded at Victor Blade and the German prisoner. "If they give you any trouble, shoot 'em." He reached out and took the Sten-gun from Harry Parsons' hand. "You know how to use this?"

"I-I'm not sure." Major Brinkley's autocratic manner had evaporated completely. He took the Sten-gun from Action Man and examined it gingerly. "I've never actually fired one!"

Action Man gently removed the gun from Brinkley's hands and gave it back to Harry Parsons. "In that case, Major, I hope you'll agree it would be better to leave Parsons in charge. He's used a Sten before . . . and he'll know what to do."

Parsons cocked the Sten and moved back a pace or two. "Blade, and you, Fritzie . . . you just step away from the others and sit down. Wouldn't want you to try to grab the Major and use him as a shield now, would we?"

The Major moved closer to Parsons, isolating Blade and the German. Action Man jerked his head at G.I. Joe and Sergeant Jackson and they glided away into the darkness.

"What's the drill?" whispered G.I. Joe.

"Two sentries in the yard near the barn where the Mark Three tanks are parked. You take 'em." Action Man's eyes glittered through the darkness. "Silently, Joe. Take 'em silently. I want those two chaps knocked out before me and Sergeant Jackson go into the farmhouse."

"If the sergeant's going in with you, he'll want this." G.I. Joe passed his carbine across to

Jackson. "I'll make do with these." He held out his bare hands.

The silhouette of the farmhouse was now in view and they sank to the ground.

"When G.I. Joe's dealt with the sentries, you and me will go into the farmhouse, Sergeant. We'll go in shooting. Sooner it's all over the better. We're gonna make a noise but let's make it as short as possible."

The sergeant seemed troubled. "Look, mate, don't think I'm scared to go in with you, but we could walk around this lot. We don't have to have a shoot-out."

"Want their guns," said Action Man shortly. "The nearer we get to Monte Carrillo, the more Germans there'll be. I doubt if we'll find an isolated group like this again."

"If they are isolated," put in G.I. Joe warningly. "I mean, we can't be sure there ain't a couple of hundred Jerries fifty yards further on."

The big British Commando nodded agreement. "I've thought of that. If there are Jerries all around us, we've had it anyway. We either get lucky here, get ourselves equipped with Jerry guns . . . an' go on to The Hill with some chance of success . . . or we lose here and now. At least, we'll go out fighting."

Both G.I. Joe and Sergeant Jackson nodded, acknowledging the force of the argument. It was all or nothing. The American asked to be given ten minutes to deal with the sentries and then vanished into the gloom. He made no sound.

The minutes ticked away. Sergeant Jackson and Action Man lay flat on the ground, eyes fixed upon the farmhouse. They had already decided to open up on anyone who came out of the farmhouse while G.I. Joe was alone.

But nothing happened. Once a burst of laughter came to them from the farmhouse windows but the door remained firmly closed. From the direction of the parked tanks there was no sound at all.

Ten minutes passed . . . twelve. Sergeant Jackson glanced enquiringly at Action Man but the big Commando smiled serenely back and held up a hand, asking for patience.

And then came a whistle. A low wolf-whistle such as the American troops used to express their admiration of a passing girl.

Action Man clapped his hand on Jackson's shoulder and they rose together, moving at a fast run, heading for the farm. Jackson veered to one side to make for the farmhouse windows and Action Man went straight for the door.

It was a flimsy door of planking with a thumb-operated latch. Six-feet-one-inch of fighting Commando hit the door squarely and smashed it wide. The shattered planks swung back and hit the inside wall with a crash and at the same moment Action Man opened fire with his Sten.

Six Germans were seated around a long wooden table with the remains of a meal spread

before them. The raking fire of the Sten-gun knocked four of them backwards off their bench seat. At the window, Sergeant Jackson's head and shoulders appeared and his carbine muzzle spurted flame, knocking over the two remaining men.

"Two more somewhere!" shouted Action Man. He leaped the bodies of the fallen Nazis and kicked open a door on the far side. Beyond he caught a glimpse of a stove, a white enamel sink and two German soldiers. One still held a piece of rag with which he'd been washing plates; the other, quicker-witted, was bending to pick up an MP40 sub-machine-gun from a corner.

The swathing fire from Action Man's Sten-gun bowled them over. The sink shattered, sending slivers of white enamel slicing in all directions.

Sergeant Jackson came in, carbine at the ready. Action Man blew out his breath in a soundless whistle and ejecting his empty Sten magazine slammed another full one in its place.

Both stood listening intently. A full minute passed but there was no noise. No sound of alarm from outside. Their assault had lasted less than a minute. They heard G.I. Joe's voice. He called. "You guys finished? I'm coming in!"

All three stood in the shattered main room of the farmhouse. Nothing stirred.

"Okay, let's collect what we came for and get out of here." Action Man began to collect the

German weapons lying on the floor. All of them had been armed with MP40's and piled in a corner were half a dozen magazine pouches. "Four guns and as much ammo as you can carry. We'll ditch the Stens and your carbine, Joe. We won't find ammo for them from here on."

* * * * *

When the sound of firing had reached the ears of Harry Parsons and the others waiting further back, Victor Blade began laughing softly.

"Shut up, you!" snapped Parsons curtly.

"There's no way you lot are going to get away with this lark, mate," grinned Blade. "I'm betting that's Jerry gun-fire you just heard. Action Man, G.I. Joe and Sergeant Jackson have all got it where the chicken got the chopper."

There was no reply from Parsons and the Major.

"So we just sit here and wait for Jerry to sneak up on us, eh?" Blade pointed at Major Brinkley. "You're going to get shot by a Jerry any minute. How does it feel, eh? And I don't suppose you've ever shot anyone in your life, have you? Never fired a gun?"

"Every officer in the British Army has fired a gun," said the Major after a while. "You're talking nonsense."

"Never been in action though, have you?"

Blade's expression was one of malevolence. "I bet you're scared out of your life."

This time the Major remained silent and in the ensuing lull they all heard a footstep. Harry Parsons slid closer to the ground and aimed his Sten-gun into the darkness.

"Parsons. You there? It's me, Sergeant Jackson!"

A collective sigh of relief was let loose as Jackson emerged from the shadows. His face was set but untroubled. "It's okay. Come up to the farmhouse, we're issuing weapons, Jerry weapons."

Major Brinkley looked at Blade with contempt. "You seem to be wrong about everything, Blade. I'd be obliged if you'd keep your mouth shut in future."

"Is that an order, cock?" Blade's grin was as aggravating as ever.

But the major made no reply. Nodding to Parsons he set off along the road to the farmhouse and the others followed.

Everyone, apart from Blade and the German prisoner, was given one of the German MP40 sub-machine-guns and pouches of spare magazines. "If you've never used one of these before, you'll find out soon enough," said Action Man grimly. He turned to the Major. "Go in there and find yourself a pair of Jerry boots that fit. And hurry it up, I want to get on."

Major Brinkley seemed to take a long time,

but when he returned he had on a pair of German jack-boots. His face was very pale but somehow his shoulders seemed to have squared off in a determined set that hadn't been there before. He'd buckled on his ammunition pouches and he'd slung his gun by its strap, across one shoulder.

"Thought you might like to sort out your own size yourself," said Action Man softly. "Okay?"

The Major nodded, his eyes holding Action Man's. "You wanted me to see what you'd done in there?"

"It's war, Major," responded Action Man grimly. "A tough war . . . and men have to be tough to fight it."

The officer nodded stiffly. "I take your point, Action Man."

"Then let's go," said the big Commando. He led the way out of the farmyard and back on to the road, heading for Monte Carrillo. He felt that he could count upon Major Brinkley to pull his weight as a soldier. The man had changed.

G.I. Joe had noticed the transformation, too. "He's beginning to find out what it's all about," he said softly. "Nothing like a little bit of action to bring people round."

"It's just a start. Before dawn breaks Major Brinkley is going to see a lot more action. An' he'll never forget it . . . if he survives!"

CHAPTER FOUR

THE HILL !

After a while they were forced to leave the road. The sky had clouded over but a pale moon rode behind the clouds and occasionally its light flooded the countryside in sudden and searching brilliance.

And the moonlight revealed to them their objective . . . Monte Carrillo . . . The Hill. It rose abruptly out of the flat plain they were crossing, dark and sinister, little more than a kilometre away. By no stretch of the imagination could it be called a mountain but Action Man estimated its height at four hundred feet. Its base was broader than its height, resembling a gigantic Christmas pudding and where the top was flattened they could make out the battered walls of what once had been an ancient castle. Time had destroyed most of the Castle of Carrillo and the R.A.F's bomber aircraft had demolished the rest in fruitless assault upon the communications brainwork inside. The entire upper third of The Hill was pock-marked with innumerable bomb-craters that linked and joined together. Not a single piece of earth at the top had not been churned up by high explosive at some time or other.

Sergeant Parsons crouched beside Action Man staring in awe at the huge dark hump. "All we have to do now . . . is get there," he muttered. Ahead, starting not two hundred metres further on were the first twisted and tangled skeins of barbed-wire fencing. It was a sea of rusting rolls of wire, five feet high and stretching back and to either side as far as they could see.

Loosely knitted, propped up at regular intervals by iron spikes, the barrier seemed impenetrable.

"Let's move nearer." Action Man rose and waved the others on and they went with him, crouching, until the wire stopped them.

"Even if we had wire-cutters, it'd take hours hacking our way through that. Must be fifty or sixty metres deep." G.I. Joe looked anxiously at Action Man. "What d'you reckon?"

"We'll go round it. There must be some way!" Action Man began to move parallel with the wire. Here and there Allied bombers had dropped their deadly cargoes on the wire and the craters could be seen but the Germans had filled in any gaps that had occurred.

Cloud obscured the moon momentarily and they pressed on in almost complete darkness.

Minutes later as they stumbled and staggered through the gloom, Blade remarked: "You know what's gonna happen, dontcha? You'll still be walking around this wire by the time it gets daylight. Ain't it occurred to anyone yet that the wire *encircles* The Hill? We could go round here forever."

"Shut up!" snapped Action Man. The thought had occurred to him a few moments earlier but he didn't want Blade to know that.

"Hey, there's water up here. Heck, it's a swamp." G.I. Joe's voice came softly back to them. The American had been leading the way and now as they concertinaed behind him, they could all feel the change in the ground. The dry, hard, dusty soil was gone. Now there were clumps of coarse reeds and it was yielding underfoot.

Obligingly the moon reappeared. The wire still grew in huge mounds to one side, but ahead the landscape had flattened. A faint milky mist clung low to the ground and reeds raised their heads through it. Here and there were patches of water that reflected the moon's soft light.

"We could get under the wire here." G.I. Joe flapped a hand at the swamp. "We'll sure get wet and muddy, but if we crawl there'll be enough space to go under."

"You'll drown first," said Blade derisively.

"We'll soon find out." Action Man jabbed his gun muzzle into Blade's back. "You go first. Move into that swamp until it's knee-deep . . . and then start crawling . . . under the wire." He turned and gestured the German prisoner forward. "You go with him. I'll be right behind."

"Do we follow?" Major Brinkley asked.

"If we three make it to the far side," Action Man nodded, "come across when I give the word."

Parsons, Sergeant Jackson, Major Brinkley and G.I. Joe sank to their haunches and watched as Action Man prodded the other two forward. They obeyed, but with reluctance.

After ten paces they were in ankle-deep water and mud. Blade stumbled and fell to his knees with a curse but rose immediately. "Keep moving," urged Action Man. "Let's get a little deeper in before we try the wire."

The water was now up to their knees and Action Man was about to give the order to crawl under the first strands when the German who had taken the lead sank from sight with the abruptness of an actor disappearing through a stage trap-door.

For a moment his arms were all they could see, fingers straining at the sky. Then his head and shoulders came up, streaming muddy water. He flung himself back, clawing for a hold. He had lost his helmet in the first unexpected immersion and his hair was flattened against his skull. He tried to scream but the mud-thickened water choked him.

Action Man pushed Blade. "Grab him, Blade. Pull him back." He pushed off the safety on his gun. "That Jerry goes under and you go

under with him."

Blade stepped cautiously forward, found a
firm foothold, and bent down, grabbing at the
German's thrashing arms. He got a hold on one
wrist and started shuffling backwards, dragging
the half-drowned Nazi with him.

The prisoner turned over on his hands and
knees in the ooze, coughing and spluttering,
wiping the slime from his face with a trembling
hand. His uniform was so mud-covered that it
was no longer possible to tell which Army he
belonged to. When he finally climbed to his feet
he looked beseechingly at Action Man with a
face which was contorted with terror.

"Please, we — we cannot go that way. We
drown. All of us. Go back . . ."

"It's the only way we can pass the wire,"
rasped Action Man. "Take it more slowly, test
each step before moving forward."

"No." The German's eyes were bright with
panic. "There are too many holes. Great pits in
the water. A man could be swallowed up."

"He's right, you know," grunted Blade
sombrely.

"There's no other way."

"Please, sir, there — there is another way!"
The German had slipped to his knees again in
the mud but he remained there, staring up at
the big British Commando. He put out one
hand in pathetic plea, fingers almost touching
Action Man's mud-covered boots. "There is a
place in the wire, further back. We passed it by

in the dark. A passage through the wire. There is only one double strand and then, beyond, a path, not very wide, to the far side."

"How do you know this?"

"Yesterday, I came through. Me and my comrades when we went to patrol out to the village. Always we come this way through the wire."

"Why don't you use the road?" put in Blade. "You're a liar."

"No." The prisoner turned desperately from one to the other. "I not lie. Ever since the invasion we do not use the road . . . because it has been mined. In — in case the Allies break through . . ."

Action Man pulled the Nazi to his feet. "Okay, I believe you. Show us how to get through the wire." The German was still festooned with the webbing belts of sub-machine-gun ammunition and Action Man tipped them with his gun muzzle as the German squelched past him. "Get those dried and cleaned soon as you like, while you're moving. When I ask for 'em, I'm going to want them in good order."

The German nodded but said nothing. But as they trudged back through the clinging mud his hands began automatically to wipe the magazine pouches free of mud. "That goes for you, too," added Action Man squinting at Blade. "Keep 'em clean."

*　　*　　*　　*　　*

The path through the wire was not elaborately camouflaged and they all wondered how they had missed noticing it when they had passed earlier.

"Just weren't looking for anything so simple," muttered G.I. Joe as he pulled aside a great loop of rusted barbed wire and exposed a path three feet wide that went through the tangled barbs as straight as a ray of sunlight.

"Let the Jerry go first," Action Man advised. "He said the roads had been mined. Maybe they decided to mine this path, too."

But the German went through the wire confidently enough and they followed, far enough behind to avoid the effects of any sudden explosion, but close enough to keep the man within range of their weapons. With every step the German took, he continued to rub his hands across the magazine pouches, drying and cleaning them. He seemed now to be content to throw in his lot with the marauding Englishmen and their American ally.

They made the crossing of the wire in total darkness but as they broke clear on the far side, the moon slid past a dark cloud and bathed the scene in white light.

The Hill was now towering above them, the first sloping rise of its broad base scarcely forty metres away. Action Man beckoned the German to him and asked: "Where's the entrance to this place. How do you get inside?"

The German aided his explanation with graphic movements of his hand. To the left, he waved his hand negatively. "That way is the road. That way is no good. Where the road is not mined there are patrols all the time. You must go the other way, right round there," he gestured again. "It is swampy, but not so bad as out there." He shuddered and looked over his shoulder at the wire. "Then round the far side you see big concrete posts and doors, big iron doors. That is the only way in and out of The Hill."

"The communications centre? The heart of the place?"

The German nodded eagerly, approvingly. "Yes. Yes the heart. It is like your heart, sir," he placed his own hand over his own heart. "The radio rooms, everything, is in the middle of The Hill."

"The middle? How do people get up and down. Are there stairs inside?"

A flash of pride showed in the man's eyes. "Not stairs, sir. Elevators. Lifts. There are four lifts. They go into the . . . heart."

"And guards? How well guarded is it?"

"Inside on the ground floor, always ten guards on duty. They are in touch by telephone and radio with all the troops outside." His arm made an all-embracing sweep. "They are on call always, of course."

"Could be worse," grinned G.I. Joe. "All

we're up against is a small mountain and half the German Army. Piece of cake!"

Action Man slapped him on the back, cheerfully. Now they had passed the wire he somehow felt Monte Carrillo was there in their grasp. Waiting for them.

"Okay, let's move round to the far side," he said. "Let's get round there and take Monte Carrillo."

Harry Parsons stepped forward. He still had the radio set on his back. He'd carried it all the way from the beach-head . . . years ago, it now seemed.

"Might as well leave the radio here Action Man. We make any signals from here and Jerry's gonna pick 'em up and trace us in no time at all. What do you think?"

"Leave it," Action Man agreed crisply. He grinned broadly at the tough sergeant. "This is where the talking stops and the fighting starts. The only equipment we want now is our guns."

"It means . . . it means we're completely cut off," said Major Brinkley with the faintest tremor in his voice. It could have been excitement . . . or fear. "Completely on our own. No hope of . . . rescue."

Action Man raised his captured German sub-machine-gun. "This is our only hope from now on, Major. A quick eye and a fast trigger-finger."

*   *   *   *   *

At approximately half-past one, the little group of ill-assorted men were in hiding among rocks and grass two hundred metres from the entrance to The Hill.

The moon had been hidden for the past half hour and judging from the lack of stars visible it appeared as though the sky was now completely covered in thick cloud. It suited Action Man well enough.

The German's description of The Hill's entrance had been accurate but the vastness of the place had taken them by surprise.

Four huge concrete pillars, each at least two metres in diameter towered halfway up the side of The Hill and the back end of The Hill had been carved out to make room for them. Between the pillars which were set thirty metres apart were two huge, riveted iron doors. They were closed now but the German assured them they opened by sliding sideways. In front of the doors the entire area was concreted in a huge flat slab. The eastern end of the slab was less than two metres in front of them. But it was not deserted. Close to the doors, as though waiting for entry, were parked four enormous petrol tankers. Two sentries walked nonchalantly to and fro.

"Do they take those inside?" asked Action Man.

The German shook his head. "No, they are parked here, under cover where the Allied guns cannot reach them. The petrol is for the Brigade vehicles out there," he moved his hand towards the blackness surrounding the Hill. "Only water supplies go inside."

"The water comes in tankers like those out there?" asked Action Man, his interest aroused suddenly.

Again the prisoner nodded. "Once a week the water comes."

"What's the German word for water?"

"*Wasser!*"

G.I. Joe came slithering along the ground beside Action Man. "What's happening, old buddy-boy? Got any ideas about getting in this place?"

"I think I have," returned Action Man thoughtfully. "I think we've had just about the biggest lucky break we could have wished for."

"What's that?" G.I. Joe was feeling the strain of waiting. "Whatever it is, let's get cracking as soon as we can." He glanced up at the sky. "It ain't going to stay like this forever. Four hours and it'll be daylight!"

"What we want, Joe, is a couple of cans of black paint." Action Man was staring at the four tankers. "How do you think we can get hold of 'em?"

"Black paint? You must be joking. What do you want that for?"

Action Man looked intently at the American. "I want black paint to paint out the petrol signs on those tankers and paint in the word Wasser. I want to turn the petrol tankers into German water tankers."

"Water tankers?"

"Yeah. Then we knock on the doors and ask to go in. Our German prisoner can speak for us. We won't fool the people inside for long . . . but for long enough, I hope."

The American took his eyes from Action Man's face and looked at the petrol tankers. Slowly, he began to grin, then he clapped Action Man on the shoulder. "I get it! We're making ourselves four big beautiful petrol bombs . . . on wheels! I like it."

"So we need black paint," said Action Man. "Where do we get it from?"

"We ain't going to find any just lying around, that's for sure. What about making some?"

Action Man shrugged. "I don't care how we get it, Joe. Make the stuff if we have to. But how?"

"It . . . it doesn't have to last long?"

"Just long enough for us to get inside The Hill . . . with the Germans thinking we're bringing in water tankers."

"We could do it with axle-grease and sump oil, I guess. Plenty of that on the tankers . . . once we've got 'em."

"Axle-grease and sump oil?" Action Man repeated the words slowly. "Yeah, it could work. It'll be a good thick black mixture, anyway. It'll have to do."

The two Commandos crawled back to their companions and explained their plan. Action

Man said: "Me and Joe will go down alone and deal with the sentries. You keep us covered. If we get in a jam, open fire but don't do that unless you have to. Once Jerry knows we're within a mile of this place, we'll have had it. Everyone understand?"

Everyone nodded and G.I. Joe said: "Okay. Let's go then."

He and Action Man began to work their way forward, keeping close to the dark, bulky shadow of The Hill, moving towards the petrol tankers and the pacing sentries.

Blade's lips moved. He said softly: "You know what's going to happen? Those two madmen are going to get us all killed."

"Shut up," hissed Sergeant Jackson. "If anyone around here's going to get killed, Blade, it's going to be you first. So you just keep quiet and do as you're told."

CHAPTER FIVE

INSIDE THE HILL!

There was no talking now when they had to, they communicated by signs and gestures.

The German sentries walked regularly to and fro — moving away from each other to the far ends of the tankers and then turning to walk back and meet in the centre. There they would stop for a moment or two, chatting in low voices, before setting out again on their routine.

Action Man and G.I. Joe arrived safely at the nearest tanker and ducked beneath the huge wheels, crawling from the first to the second. There they lay motionless as the sentries met and halted. The jack-boots of the two men were inches from them.

Action Man tapped G.I. Joe on the shoulder and they rose to their full height. The Nazis, rifles slung over their shoulders, were talking softly and whatever it was they were saying was never completed.

Action Man's left arm came around the throat of one German and his right hand slammed hard against the back of the man's

helmet, forcing his chin forward and down over the encircling fore-arm. Two paces away, G.I. Joe was doing the same thing.

It was over in seconds. The bodies of the sentries sagged limply in the grasp of the two fighting men and they were lowered to the ground and dragged away behind the tankers. The sudden assault had been completely soundless.

Action Man waved his arm and Sergeant Jackson, Harry Parsons and Major Brinkley came quickly towards him, prodding Blade and the German prisoner before them.

"Sump oil and Axle-grease. There'll be tool kits somewhere. In the driving cabs probably. Let's get our make-shift paint made."

They had no trouble getting the ingredients they wanted. They mixed the oil and grease together in their helmets. It was as black and sticky a mixture as Action Man could have wished.

He handed one of the filled helmets to Blade. "Get up top and start painting," he ordered. "You'll make a nice target up there if anyone sees you so the quicker you get the job done, the sooner you can come down. Use your hands. Smear this stuff over the existing petrol signs and write Wasser beneath. Do it as neatly as you can, neatly enough to fool anyone who's not taking a real close look. Okay?"

Blade replied with an unrecognisable mumble, partly protest, but he swung up on to the driving cab step and from there on to the rounded body of the tanker.

Action Man handed another helmet-full of the mixture to Major Brinkley and told him what he wanted done, then he took the arm of the German prisoner and led him behind the end tanker.

"What do we have to do to get 'em to open up inside?"

The German was thoroughly uneasy. "The people in The Hill know if supplies are arriving. Always there is a telephone message to them first."

Action Man called softly to Sergeant Jackson and Harry Parsons. "Search around, lads. There are telephone wires leading inside somewhere. Find 'em . . . and cut 'em." He turned his attention back to the German. "How many ways are there of getting up into the communications centre where the radio and observation posts are?"

"Just the four lifts."

"There must be stairs of some sort."

"Yes, one flight of stairs," the prisoner agreed reluctantly. "They lead from the room where the guards are on duty."

Blade had worked fast, spurred on by Action Man's hint that he made a good target on top of the tanker. The petrol signs had been obliterated and above was the word WASSER.

"Now get on with the tanker behind. Have you got enough of that goo left?"

Blade held up his helmet with a hand that dripped thick streams of the sticky mess. "With what's in this helmet and what I've got on my hand and up my arm, I could paint words over every vehicle in the German Army," he growled. "I've got enough, mate."

Major Brinkley too had been working fast. He had finished one tanker and was already starting on the second. Only five minutes had passed since the attack on the two sentries.

But Action Man was anxious. Every passing second made their venture more hazardous. He realized there were dozens of unforeseen events which could happen to ruin all the good work they'd achieved so far.

The sentries must be changed at some time or another. They wouldn't be on duty all night. Even now a relief section might be marching through the night towards them. They had to get inside The Hill . . . and fast!

When all four tankers had been hastily disguised as water-tankers, Action Man urged the German prisoner up behind the driving wheel of the leading vehicle. To Sergeant Jackson and Harry Parsons he gave the coal-scuttle helmets taken from the sentries.

"Wear these. At least you'll look like Germans. We only need to fool the guys inside for a short while."

He turned to G.I. Joe. "You drive the last truck, Joe . . . have Blade aboard with you. And keep moving. If things look like going wrong, keep driving. I want all four of these tankers inside."

"You can't keep me out, buddy," responded the American laconically.

The British Commando swung into the cab of the leading lorry and settled himself beside the German. "I'm going to bang on that door and get someone to answer," he told him. "When they want to know what's happening, you tell them you have orders to deliver water. You've been told to do it at night because of the fear of Allied bombing during the day. And if they say they've got all the water they need . . . tell 'em they've got to have more. Now, start the engine and drive up real close."

The German did as he was told. Action Man dropped to the ground leaving the cab door open, and walked to the tanker behind. Sergeant Jackson, grim-faced beneath the shadow of his German helmet sat waiting. Action Man said:

"Did you find the phone wires?"

"Yeah. Me and Parsons ripped 'em out."

"You know what we're going to do? We're driving inside The Hill as soon as the doors open. All four tankers. Then we take the guards. Start shooting as soon as you see a target inside. I don't want too many shots fired back at us . . . because if they put a bullet into these tankers . . . you're gonna get roasted. We'll all roast. Understand?"

"I get you."

Action Man nodded: "Make sure he knows the score, too." He pointed at Major Brinkley seated beside the sergeant and then walked back to tell the driver behind.

*   *   *   *   *

All four tankers' engines were now running. The drivers sat staring at Action Man as he banged upon the iron doors of The Hill with the butt of his MP40. The noise seemed deafening.

Several seconds elapsed before a small eye-level peep-hole slid back and they heard the guttural tones of a German. The voice sounded surprised.

Action Man stood to one side, his back against the steel door and, raising his sub-machine-gun, aimed it deliberately at the head of the German prisoner seated behind the wheel of the leading tanker. The distance between him and Action Man's gun was too slight to give the faintest hope of a miss.

"Four water tankers. Let us in," said the German hoarsely. He had been carefully instructed in his lines and he strove to repeat accurately what Action Man had taught him. "We tried to telephone you we were coming but the lines are down."

This was the moment when Action Man knew his plan could fail. But it was a chance he had deliberately taken. If water tankers had arrived only the day before, or two days earlier, the arrival of four more tankers would seem extremely suspicious to the Germans inside. He was banking upon them not having had their water replenished for at least three days.

He could hear a conversation going on inside. Someone was agreeing that the telephones were out of order. Then a voice said: "The water tankers are not due until tomorrow."

Action Man wiped the perspiration from his brow. It was going to succeed.

The peep-hole became a shadow as someone moved against it on the other side of the door. "Why are you early?"

The German prisoner bit his lip before answering. "We have orders to deliver in darkness . . . because of the risk of Allied bombers tomorrow."

The peep-hole vanished as the cover was drawn across it. And then came the subdued murmur of hidden machinery and Action Man became aware of the door at his back beginning to glide sideways. He felt like cheering.

Instead, he raced around the front of the leading tanker and climbed swiftly up into the cab beside the prisoner. Lights inside The Hill had been turned down. Blue bulbs high in the lofty ceiling cast just sufficient illumination to reveal an enormous open area supported here and there by giant concrete pillars. On the far side facing them were four small doors. The doors of the lifts, thought Action Man. And it looks as though all the lifts are on an upper floor.

The huge double metal doors were now wide open and a German soldier was beckoning them forward, gesturing to a position to his right, obviously directing them to the connections for the water supplies.

"Move forward, take it slowly," Action Man whispered, his gun held towards his driver. "Go the way the guy is telling you, but move right across to the far side. Give those behind room to get in."

The German was frightened. His hand on the gear lever trembled to such an extent he could hardly control it. But he managed to engage first gear and the tanker rumbled forward. Action Man silently blessed the dim light which would partly conceal the crude painting on the tanker's side. Anyone looking at the "Wasser tanker" might be puzzled, but in this light, they wouldn't be sure anything was wrong.

As the tanker moved inside The Hill, Action Man glanced backwards. The other tankers were following, barely a foot of space separated one from the other.

They were parking now on the far side. The German soldier had turned his attention to the second and third vehicles which were crowding in. He began to wave his arms and shout angrily. "Not this side. Only two here . . . the other two on the other side!"

Sergeant Jackson's tanker was drawn up beside Action Man's. The British Commando gestured and he and Jackson slipped down from their cabs. Major Brinkley followed a moment later. The towering side of the bulk-carrier hid them from the view of the guard.

The throbbing of the tankers' engines made a crescendo of sound inside the lofty space, a noise that seemed to bounce off the concrete walls and crash against their ears.

The fourth tanker, driven by G.I. Joe, was half in and half out of the doors. The German directing operations marched toward the cab angrily. He pulled open the cab door and G.I. Joe's booted foot hit him squarely in the face. At the same time, the American revved the engine and drove the tanker fully inside.

A loud German voice echoed around the cavern. Demanding. A voice tinged with exasperation. It came from a loud-speaker on the wall.

"What's he say?" Action Man gripped his prisoner by the arm. "What's he saying?"

"He is asking if everything is in? Can he shut the doors?"

"Tell him yes. Shout it!"

The prisoner made the reply and the iron doors rolled back, shutting out the night. They were inside with four fully loaded petrol tankers. So far not a shot had been fired.

Everyone was out of the tankers now and Action Man gestured them to spread out around the walls. Suddenly the blue lights overhead went out to be replaced at once by the light from a dozen brilliant fluorescent tubes. It lit the area more vividly than daylight.

"Where are the guards' quarters?"

The prisoner shook his head. "I do not know, sir." He muttered. He flapped an arm around uncertainly. "Over there, I should think!"

"Call 'em!" snapped Action Man. "Call out. Tell them there's something wrong and to come down at the double."

The prisoner's face sagged disbelievingly. Action Man prodded him in the back with his gun-muzzle. "Tell 'em to come down here! Now."

For a split second a gleam appeared in the German's eye. Then he cried loudly: "Guard. Turn out!" He yelled a lot more, words which Action Man could not follow, so rapidly did the man speak. But he was still shouting when there came the clatter of jack-booted feet and five Germans tumbled down an iron staircase at the extreme end of the cavern.

A shot rang out, and the German prisoner fell back and collapsed. At the same moment Action Man yelled, "Fire!" and the small assault force brought their entire fire-power to bear upon the entering guards.

The men on the metal stair-case were slammed back against the concrete wall as a score of bullets thudded into them and then they toppled headfirst down the steps to the ground.

Action Man sprinted across the open space to

the steps, leaping over the bodies. "More of 'em up here. Follow me!"

By the time he reached the door at the top, G.I. Joe was at his heels. They went in together, firing from the hip, raking the room beyond.

The room was empty. A door on the far side swung slowly open and they raced across to it. There was a flight of cold concrete steps leading up. At the top of the stairs a German guard was pulling the string from the handle of a stick-grenade. Behind him a sergeant and another soldier were squinting down the barrels of sub-machine-guns.

Action Man slammed G.I. Joe back from the door and swung it hard shut. They heard the thud as the hand-grenade fell against it.

"Cover me." Action Man threw himself flat, pulling open the door in the same movement. The hand grenade rolled through the open door and a hail of bullets whined through the air above him. Then G.I. Joe's MP40 opened up. He too was lying full length, spraying bullets up the staircase. Action Man grabbed the grenade and flipped it back up the stairs and swivelling around on his back, kicked the door shut.

The blast from the exploding grenade forced the door off its hinges and jets of smoke and cement dust spouted out through the cracks.

As one man, Action Man and G.I. Joe ejected their spent magazines and slammed new ones home. There was space to one side of the door, where the hinges had been, and they pushed

their gun muzzles through. They both squeezed the triggers. There was no need to aim in the confined space of the staircase, their bullets ricocheted to and fro a dozen times. Anyone standing inside must have been viciously cut down.

Before they opened the door properly, they again reloaded. But the precaution was unnecessary. The grenade had exploded in mid-air as Action Man had thrown it back. The three Germans lay on the stairs unmoving. It was obvious they were dead.

"Major Brinkley, come here." Action Man walked to the door and yelled. When the major appeared at the foot of the iron staircase, he said: "Come up here and sit in this room. Just sit and watch that staircase. If anyone or anything comes down, start shooting. Don't bother to see what it is. Shoot it. Okay?"

Major Brinkley entered the bullet-scarred room and looked speechlessly at the bodies lying on the stairs. But he nodded briskly enough and took up a position on the far side of the room facing the door. He held his sub-machine-gun ready in both hands.

"You sure you can use that?" asked Action Man.

The major nodded. Then he said, "I can use it. I've shot someone."

"Shot someone?" Action Man and G.I. Joe echoed the words together. "Who the heck did you shoot?" asked G.I. Joe in amazement.

"Our—our German prisoner." The words came from Major Brinkley's lips falteringly. "When you told him to call out, he was warning the Germans that we were waiting." He took a deep shuddering breath. "I shot him!"

"Yeah. There was a shot, just at the moment you yelled out, 'fire'," exclaimed G.I. Joe.

"How'd you know he was warning his pals?"

"I-I can speak German," the major muttered. "Quite well."

G.I. Joe and Action Man exchanged glances and then Action Man said: "Okay, Major. Well, just keep watching that door as I told you."

He and G.I. Joe went back to the petrol tankers. Sergeant Jackson and Harry Parsons were standing by the four lift doors Action Man had noticed earlier. All four doors were open and the lift cages were on the ground level.

"Thought we'd better get these down," grinned Sergeant Jackson. "Didn't want a lot of Krauts from upstairs descending on us. Didn't think it would work . . . but I just pressed the buttons and down they came."

Action Man nodded approvingly. He turned to the others. "Now we've got work to do. We've got to fix a time-fuse so we can blow up these tankers. When they all go up together inside here," he looked all around at the huge concrete cavern. "It should make a fair old bang!"

There was a long silence. Then Blade said harshly: "And when this 'fair old bang' happens . . . where are we gonna be? We better be a long way away, mate . . . or we're going to cop it, too." He flung out an arm toward the tankers. "You blow that lot up and you'll blow this whole mountain to pieces! And what about getting out of here, anyway? Those doors are shut, mate. How do we open them?"

Action Man regarded him coldly. "You do as you're told, Blade. And keep quiet."

"Sounds like you're chicken to me, chum," put in G.I. Joe. "I'm personally all for tying you into the cab of one of these things and leaving you behind anyway."

There was a sudden burst of sub-machine-gun fire and Major Brinkley shouted, "Someone tried to come down the stairs. I got him."

"We'd better get moving here," said Action Man. "The guys upstairs may not be able to telephone anyone right now. But they must be sure as eggs using their radio gear to call for help!"

He swung round on G.I. Joe. "Okay, Joe, let's start on that little trick you told me about. Let's fix our fuses."

G.I. Joe winked. He seemed quite unconcerned. "I want the shirts off your backs, lads. Then I want you to tear 'em into strips; then I want you to fix the strips together to make one nice long piece of material. If there's enough of that black paint left, you can use that. It'll stick your shirt material. Or make a hole in the end of each strip and connect 'em together with a smaller piece of material. I don't care how you do it . . . but do it. Your lives depend upon it. Four long pieces . . . go to it, lads."

Sergeant Jackson, Harry Parsons, G.I. Joe himself, and Blade began to tear their shirts into four-inch wide strips. Action Man went from tanker to tanker unscrewing the inspection covers on the top of each. The smell of petrol filled the cavern with its sickly fumes.

Then Action Man noticed a stack of jerry-cans in a shadowy corner. One or two were filled with water but the rest were empty. It gave him an idea and, drawing petrol from one tanker, he quickly filled all the cans.

"What's this? Something new, buddy?" called G.I. Joe, his fingers still busy as he plaited the torn ends of a shirt together. "A refinement?"

Action Man carried the jerry-cans of petrol towards the lift cages and began stacking them inside. There were enough cans to make a considerable pile in each lift. "A little something for whoever's upstairs. Maybe it'll quieten 'em before they tell what's happened."

G.I. Joe looked doubtful. "How are you going to send the lifts up?"

The British Commando walked past the lifts and tapped a hatch cover in the wall. "What's the betting there's hand-winding gear in here . . . to raise or lower the lifts if one of 'em gets stuck in mid-shaft. There's always an emergency winding gear somewhere."

G.I. Joe had finished making a long length of material from his shirt and he draped it carefully over the open door of one of the tanker cabs. He delved further inside and fumbled with a tool kit, extracting a screw-driver. "Okay, buddy-boy, let's take a look."

The screws around the hatch came out easily. Inside a huge protruding hexagonal nut and beneath it, held by spring clamps, was an equally huge iron handle. He pulled the handle out. It was like a gigantic car-starter handle. "Let's see if it works."

The handle fitted the hexagonal nut snugly. G.I. Joe and Action Man threw their weight into turning the handle. The lift cages rose slightly.

"Okay, so it works." Action Man stopped winding. "Let's fix a fuse on the jerry-cans and send 'em up."

"Don't want too long a fuse," G.I. Joe said reflectively. "Just enough for us to get the lifts up the shaft." He stepped inside one of the lifts and climbed on top of the jerry-cans. Putting his hands to his eyes to shut out the light he squinted up the shaft above. "Looks like twelve metres of shaft. Let's make it a short fuse and wind as fast as we can."

It was a rough and ready scheme but the only one they could think of.

G.I. Joe looked at Action Man. "You're the only one with a shirt, so let's have it, buddy-boy."

When the shirt had been torn into suitable lengths, G.I. Joe took off the cap of one jerry-can in each lift-cage. Then he inserted one end of the shirt strip into the can and into the petrol. The shirt material began to soak up the petrol and they could see the darkening stain as it worked its way down the cloth.

G.I. Joe lit a match and applied it to the lower end of the strip of cotton. It burned dully, slowly, but didn't go out, gradually climbing up toward the dark petrol-stained area.

"Once it gets up there . . . whoooosh!" snapped G.I. Joe. "Come on lads. Light the other strips and then lets get winding. We're running out of time."

As soon as the four strips of shirt material had been lit, G.I. Joe and Action Man slammed the lift doors and flung themselves to the winding handle.

Through the cracks of the closed doors they could see the lift cages slowly ascending.

"Heck, I thought they'd go up faster than this." The American was streaming perspiration from his exertions. "The darned things will blow up before we get 'em to the top."

"Save your breath and wind this handle." Action Man was streaming with perspiration, too. The muscles in his arms bulged with the effort, but he kept going.

There came a tremendous explosion behind them.

"That's not our petrol cans!" G.I. Joe kept

winding but he and Action Man turned to stare behind. A billowing cloud of smoke and dust was belching out of the door of the room where Major Brinkley was on guard.

"Jackson, take over this winding." The sergeant seized the handle and Action Man, snatching up his MP40 ran to the iron staircase. "Major Brinkley! Major . . . you okay in there?"

The room was still hazy with drifting dust. Major Brinkley was sitting slumped against the far wall. His clothes were torn in several places and his voice when he spoke was very weak. "They . . . threw a hand grenade down the stairs. No one followed it up. I-I've still got their stairs covered." He moved the muzzle of his gun waveringly. "Got 'em covered."

"You're hit!" Action Man squatted beside the Major. "Where?"

"In the leg. I-I can't stand."

"Can you move at all?"

"Not—not too well." Major Brinkley's eyes were riveted on the debris-littered staircase through the door. "Don't worry, no one will come down those stairs, I promise." He was obviously in pain and winced as he tried to ease his position.

Action Man was trying to think of words of comfort when a deafening explosion rocked the room, dust clouds billowed out from the concrete walls. Both men ducked involuntarily and then a second, third and fourth explosion made shock waves bounce off the walls.

The jerry-cans of petrol in the lift-cages, thought Action Man, his ears ringing with the deafening sound. If they went off on the upper floor, there's going to be one heck of a mess up there.

"Did—did you do that?" asked the Major softly. "Those explosions?"

Action Man nodded. "I'll get someone up here to take your place, Major."

"No. I'm all right." Without moving his head, he added, "There's a lever over there, behind that desk. It operates the opening and closing the main doors." A smile passed fleetingly over his face. "There's a list of operating instructions printed beside it . . . in German . . . easy enough to read. When—when you want to leave, Action Man, let me know. I'll open the doors for you . . . and close them behind you."

"And close them?"

Major Brinkley's face was set. "I-I don't think I'll be leaving with you, not with this leg." He touched his chest with one hand. "There—there's a chunk of grenade splinter in here, too. I'm not going to go far. You'll get a better explosion with the doors shut. The blast will all go up. Okay?"

"That makes good sense," Action Man agreed. "But we're not leaving you here, sir. You came in with us and you're going out with us. If all goes well we can get you medical attention by dawn. Don't worry, you'll make it." He nodded at the door which led to the upper floor. "You sure you can hold out here?"

"I'm sure." The Major fixed his eye across the room and raised his sub-machine-gun. He held it quite steadily. "You can go."

Action Man hurried back down the iron staircase. G.I. Joe and Sergeant Jackson were working busily beside the four tankers. Four long strips of shirt material were hanging from the open inspection hatches on each of the tankers. The strips hung down almost to the wheels.

From above came the rustling, crackling sound of flames.

"I think we started a fire up there," grinned G.I. Joe, noticing Action Man's expression. "Those lift shafts are acting as chimneys now, sending a nice draught up there. They're really in trouble."

"Okay, let's give 'em more trouble. Let's blow up these tankers."

G.I. Joe lit a match and held it under the first strip of shirt material. "Now?"

"Now!" nodded the British Commando grimly. Raising his voice, he called, "While G.I. Joe's lighting the fuses, the rest of you get over against the doors. They'll open soon. When they do, get out fast and make your way around The Hill, we'll go back the way we came. But all of you get moving fast . . . there may be unfriendly people arriving outside at any moment." He jerked his thumb at the roof. "Depends how much those guys up there managed to put out over the air before we blew 'em up."

He pointed at Blade whilst looking at Sergeant Jackson. "Give him a gun and ammo, sergeant. If we've got to fight our way out, he can shoot as well as the rest of us and we'll need all the firepower we can muster."

To Blade, he said: "If you use that gun on anyone or anything except the enemy, Blade, I'll cut you down myself."

"All four fuses alight," called G.I. Joe. "Five minutes before this lot blows."

"Over by the doors, then, all of you." Action Man ran to the iron-staircase. "Remember, clear out as soon as they open."

Inside the grenade-ravaged room, Major Brinkley was still keeping guard on the inner staircase. He had dragged himself behind the desk and a trail of blood showed the agony of his movement.

"Pull the switch, Major. We're leaving. We've got less than five minutes. And you're coming with me. If you can't walk, I'll carry you."

Major Brinkley leaned against the switch in the wall and the low rumble of the opening doors came to their ears. "I think I'll stay as I said, Action Man . . . and close the doors for you."

"Those four tankers will do enough damage, doors open or closed," replied Action Man crisply. "I'm taking you out, Major."

"No." Major Brinkley's voice was now so low, Action Man could scarcely hear him. "I'm staying." He took away the hand he had held against his chest while he was speaking. His shirt was stained with blood. He raised his eyes to meet Action Man's. "I-I'm not fit to travel."

"You'll make it, sir."

From somewhere inside himself, the Major drew on reserves of energy. He raised himself into a more upright position against the wall. His face was chalky white but his voice was surprisingly firm.

"I said I'm not fit to travel. I'll remain here. You leave at once, Action Man. Get out. That's an order!"

Still Action Man hesitated and the Major said again, slowly but very clearly, "That is an order!" He coughed and there was blood at the corner of his mouth.

Action Man rose slowly to his feet. At the door he turned to face Major Brinkley. He brought his right foot slamming down beside his left, rigidly to attention, and his right arm rose stiffly, finger-tips extended in military salute.

As he ran to the open doors he just had time to notice the four strips of shirt material were burned three-quarters of the way up to the tanker inspection hatches and glowing brightly. Soon the glow would reach the darkened, petrol-soaked area and then there would be flame . . . flame moving faster . . . racing to the top and into the huge tanks containing thousands of gallons of inflammable liquid!

Outside the darkness was as impenetrable as ever. The great doors began to move, closing behind him. Action Man ran and almost blundered into G.I.Joe.

"Just waiting to make sure you got out, buddy," said the American. He looked past Action Man. "Where's the Major?"

"Stayed behind," replied Action Man shortly. "C'mon, let's move."

They were just rounding the far end of The Hill when distinctly to their ears came the sound of moving vehicles. The rattle and clatter of tanks.

"The Jerries in The Hill must have got out a call for help after all," murmured G.I. Joe. "Arriving just in time to see the fireworks, I'd say."

"Keep going," advised Action Man. "We've a way to travel."

They were beginning to wade through the swampy area short of the barbed wire when The Hill blew up.

The blast threw them to the ground. Wave upon wave of deafening sound beat at their ears. The earth beneath their bodies moved as though an earthquake was taking place. Boulders and rocks and great earthy chunks of grass fell around them and on them until they were half-buried.

When the debris stopped falling they looked up at The Hill which had been behind them. It

had disappeared and in its place stood a huge area of smoking rubble. It seemed to stretch out endlessly.

"The Major was in there?" said G.I. Joe in awe.

"Yes," said Action Man. "He was."

CHAPTER SIX

MAKING IT BACK!

Sergeant Jackson and Harry Parsons were waiting at the gap in the wire. Parsons had retrieved his radio-set from the place where he'd left it and was crouching with it strapped on his back.

"The Jerries are out in force," said Action Man, dropping down with G.I. Joe beside the other two. "It's going to be tough getting back."

Parsons said: "Shall I make a signal to Eagle Base? Let 'em know the good news?"

"Not worth it. They probably heard the bang and if they didn't aerial reconnaissance in the morning will soon show 'em what's happened. And if Jerry picks up our signal, he'll be down on us like a dog on a bone."

G.I. Joe jerked his thumb behind to where The Hill had been. "Maybe they haven't got any radio gear left. That place ain't operating, that's for sure."

"Where's Blade?" Action Man looked at Sergeant Jackson questioningly. "He got out of

The Hill?"

"Came out with the rest of us," agreed the veteran sergeant. "But we all got our heads down and ran, like you said. Split up in the dark, but I thought we'd all meet here."

"We have," said Action Man slowly, glancing around as he spoke. "We've all met here . . . except Blade."

"Reckon Jerry got him?"

The big Commando shook his head. "I don't think so. We'd have seen more of 'em around if they'd taken a prisoner . . . or shot someone. They'd be looking for us, too."

"Maybe he's still making his way here. He could have got lost in the dark."

"We'll give him another couple of minutes. Then we go through the wire."

As they waited they heard again the rumble of moving vehicles. From the volume of sound, Action Man judged the Germans to be moving a great number of men and armour.

After a further space of time he jerked his head at the others. "Let's go. We can't wait any longer."

"Maybe he's already through the wire," suggested Harry Parsons. "I wouldn't put it past him to just keep going. He wouldn't wait around for us if he'd got here first."

They crossed the wire safely and went on and Action Man set a course which he considered to be a repeat of the route by which they'd arrived earlier. Fortunately, the sky was still filled with

cloud and the darkness was almost total. He
gestured for Sergeant Jackson to take the lead
and dropped back to talk to G.I. Joe.

His voice was anxious as he said: "I think
Blade came through the wire ahead of us, Joe."

"And skedaddled off on his own?" the
American said.

"Yeah. He's out there somewhere. With a
sub-machine-gun and half a dozen loaded
magazines."

"He'll be able to take care of himself then."

"He may be thinking of taking care of us."
Action Man's face was set in hard lines and his
eyes were bleak. "It won't take Blade long to
realise that if he gets rid of us four . . . there
won't be anyone left to spread the word about
him being an escaped prisoner. All he'd have to
do is pretend he'd got separated from his unit.
No one's going to ask too many questions out
here with a battle going on. Or he could just
hide himself away, maybe until the war is over."

The American grimaced. "So we don't just
have to watch out for Jerry . . . we have to keep
an eye open for Blade too."

"I think he'll be around, not far away, looking for a chance to wipe us out."

"I'll mention it to the others," muttered G.I.
Joe. "Heck, this is a problem we could have
done without."

The thought of Blade with his wolfish grin,
possibly stalking them in the darkness put them
all on edge. But they moved forward without

running into trouble and as the first grey streaks of dawn's light touched the sky they were within sight of the devastated village of Tavati.

They approached the village in a flanking movement from one side. "We'll hide out here until tomorrow night," said Action Man. "We'll send a signal to Eagle Base, telling our position. Without The Hill pin-pointing targets for the German guns, our boys may be breaking out from the beach-head in force during the day, they may even be in Tavati with us before the day's out."

It was a good plan which all four approved and when they reached the jumbled ruins they quickly made a strong-point from which they could defend themselves if the Germans moved up.

They chose a house in the village centre, digging themselves in, building ramparts from the debris. By the time the sun began to rise over the horizon they felt themselves to be able to withstand any attack which might be made. At least, for a few hours.

Harry Parsons rigged up his radio set and called Eagle Base. Almost immediately he received a reply.

"Eagle Base to Eagle One. Good to hear you. Stand by for a signal from General Morecombe."

Static hissed and spluttered in the earphones. Harry Parsons turned to Action Man and raised his thumb to signify he had established contact and as he did so there came the clattering of a sub-machine-gun.

A look of surprise and dismay came over the radio man's face and he fell back against the set. Another burst of fire and the radio itself jerked and twisted and fell sideways. The long aerial snapped off short and the sound of static ceased abruptly.

"Where'd it come from? Did you see anything?" Action Man crouched behind the defensive brickwork they'd thrown up. G.I. Joe knelt there with his MP40 held ready, searching for a target.

"I was looking at Harry," the American confessed, "but the shots must have come from over there." He nodded at the desolate jumble of fallen masonry littering the street. "Maybe near that end house where we found the others in the cellar."

Suddenly they stared at each other. "Blade!" whispered Action Man. He glanced back at Harry Parsons who was being attended by Sergeant Jackson. "He shot out the radio-set . . . so we wouldn't be able to radio back anything about it."

Harry Parsons had a shattered shoulder but Jackson had used a field-dressing on it which had stopped the bleeding. The radio set was finished. The half-dozen bullets had smashed it completely.

There was more trouble. G.I. Joe touched Action Man's shoulder and pointed off across the fields. A long line of men in field-grey uniforms were advancing steadily towards the village. The rising sun glinted occasionally on rifle barrels and coal-scuttle helmets. They were less than three hundred metres distant.

"Looks as though they mean to occupy this ruin and use it as a defence line," muttered Action Man. "There's one good thing about it. Jerry must think our lads will break out of the beach-head. They've given up relying on their artillery to stop 'em. They're going to fight it out with infantry."

"And we'll be caught in the middle," added G.I. Joe. He chuckled. "Well, ol' buddy-boy, looks like it's going to be another busy day."

"I wish we'd told Eagle Base we were here before the radio went out of action," said Action Man. "They might have got help to us."

* * * * *

On the other side of the street, among the ruined houses, Private Victor Blade had seen the advancing German infantry too. He'd been about to work his way around Action Man's defence position to a point where he could fire another burst at the four men. As Action Man had deduced, Blade's intention was to wipe out his erstwhile companions; the only witnesses to him being a prisoner on a murder charge.

But the German infantry changed all that. He licked his lips nervously, pressing himself into the rubble. Looking back over his shoulder he could see the wrecked Town Hall where he'd been locked in the cellar with Major Brinkley and Sergeant Jackson.

"I'll hole up there," he thought. "If I can pull a few bricks and planks down across the door, no one will know I'm there. It's the only chance I've got anyway."

*   *   *   *   *

Harry Parsons propped himself up against the bricks and laid his sub-machine-gun on top. His face was pale but he managed a grin. "I can shoot okay," he told the others.

Action Man nodded approval. Sergeant Jackson and G.I. Joe were also waiting, ready. The German infantry were no more than fifty metres away. They came on unconcernedly, talking and calling to each other. Most of them were armed with rifles but here and there along the line were men with Spandau machine-guns.

At twenty metres they began to slow as they started to climb over the scattered bricks. Action Man raised his MP40 and the others did the same.

"Concentrate on the guys with the Spandaus!"

At the same moment, they all commenced firing a vicious scything stream of bullets that tore holes in the German line. The Germans, taken completely by surprise seemed unable to realise what was happening. Those that weren't hit continued to move forward, bewildered.

Empty magazines fell in a clattering heap at the feet of the four men as they ejected the empties and replaced them.

And the German line broke. The grey-clad men turned and began to run in panic, racing away from the withering fire that had decimated their ranks.

Action Man stopped firing. The four looked at each other in satisfaction.

"Gave 'em something to think about," said G.I. Joe with his usual grin.

"Be okay if I nip out there and find a few water-bottles?" asked Sergeant Jackson. He inclined his head at the sun which was now riding higher in the sky. "If it's as hot as it was yesterday, we'll need 'em."

"Yeah. Good idea," Action Man agreed. Harry Parsons was leaning back against the brickwork breathing heavily. "You okay, Harry?"

The radio-man nodded gamely. "I'll manage," he replied.

"Don't forget Blade," cautioned G.I. Joe. "He's behind us somewhere."

"Gone to ground, I'd say," said Action Man. "He won't show himself while Jerry's around."

"What happens now? They'll come again, I guess."

"Maybe, maybe not. They can't know how many of us there are here. For all they know there may be a couple of hundred Allied troops hidden here. My guess is they'll bring up mortars and give us a good going over before the infantry advance again."

"So we wait."

"So we wait," echoed Action Man.

The mortar shells began to fall around them ten minutes later. They came screaming in out of the air and burst with deafening explosions. But the main danger was from the flying chunks of brickwork that they threw up.

The Germans plastered the ruins of the village from end to end and when the mortaring stopped, the infantry came forward. This time they advanced in short, sharp rushes, dropping to the ground every few yards, then rising and running in again. And the machine-gunners had been ordered out to the flanks where they kept up an intermittent fire, searching for targets.

Although not directed at their defence position, the machine-gun fire made Action Man and his comrades keep their heads well down. This time they could hear the gasping breath of the running infantrymen, scarcely ten metres away, before they poked their heads above the bricks and opened fire.

The four MP40's cut the Germans down like tall grass before a mower. But Sergeant Jackson was hit. He fell to the ground with a gasp, blood spurting from his right hand where a bullet had gone through.

."It—it came from behind," grunted the veteran, pulling out a handkerchief and binding it over the wound. "They're behind us."

G.I. Joe stood up and Action Man was with him shoulder-to-shoulder. A continuous flash of flame sprang from their gun muzzles as they fired from the hip, bowling over half a dozen Germans who had worked in behind them across the street. Before he fell, one of them threw a hand grenade and although it exploded against their brick and masonry defence works, the blast knocked Action Man and G.I. Joe to the ground.

"Look out, they're coming again!" Harry Parsons, the only one standing, began to fire a long burst. "Come on! They're here."

G.I. Joe and Action Man scrambled to their feet. Half a dozen Germans, bayonets fixed, were almost upon them. Harry Parsons shot two of them. G.I. Joe accounted for two more but the others leaped down into the small defence post.

A bayonet lunged at Action Man as he rolled away from it and grabbed the rifle barrel at the same time. A quick jerk and the German staggered towards him, off balance, to run into a hay-making right-hand punch that dropped him instantly. The British Commando fell with the German and kicked out with the sole of his boot at the second German's knee. The man screamed in agony and collapsed, dropping his rifle, clasping his hands to his leg.

"We can't clutter up this place with prisoners," grunted G.I. Joe. He grasped both Germans by their collars and almost threw them over the defence-works. "Get outa here, you lucky coupla Krauts! We don't wantcha!"

The Germans, amazed at their good fortune, scrambled away as fast as they could go, the one with the damaged knee hobbling like an old man with rheumatism.

Mortar shells began to drop close at hand. Lumps of red-hot metal fragments screamed through the air close to their heads. Action Man banged a fresh magazine into his gun. "Last one, lads! How many rounds you got left?"

"I'm on my last."

"And me."

Harry Parsons didn't answer. He had slumped sideways against the bricks. He was breathing heavily.

"I—I'm all right," he gasped as G.I. Joe bent over him. "Just a bit tired. Lemme alone . . . okay."

"They'll charge again when the mortaring stops," sighed Action Man. "Could be we won't stop 'em this time." He winked at G.I. Joe and slapped Sergeant Jackson on the shoulder. "Been nice knowing you guys. Couldn't wish for better men to fight with."

A dark shadow flashed across the wrecked village and immediately after came the screaming roar of aircraft engines. Above the noise of the engines, the steady bang-bang-bang of

cannon shells.

G.I. Joe raised his head. "Yanks!" He took off his helmet and hurled it into the air. "Look at them. Mustangs! Boy, what a beautiful sight!"

Swooping low across the fields, racing away from them, were three Mustang fighter planes, the white star of the Allied Air Forces emblazoned on their wings. As Action Man and Sergeant Jackson joined G.I. Joe, watching, the three planes zoomed up in a wing-breaking climb before banking and taking up formation line astern. They turned and came back at the village. Brilliant lights began to dance along the leading edges of their wings.

"Get down! They're firing at us!" G.I. Joe flung himself to the ground and the others fell on top of him. Cannon shells smashed into the debris around them.

Half a dozen times the three planes attacked the village before climbing once more . . . and flying away. The four men in the battered defensive position raised themselves from the ground and shook their heads, trying to shake the echoes of the air attack from their heads.

"What next?" grunted Sergeant Jackson. "Blade, the Germans and now our own Air Forces. They're all trying to get us."

Harry Parsons had managed to drag himself into an upright position and now he stared dully down the street. "This is it. We've had it this time. Blooming hundreds of 'em! Look!"

The other three took up their weapons and faced the newcomers. It was obvious to them all that this was an attack they wouldn't be able to beat off. Men were swarming everywhere, clambering over the wrecked houses, running up the debris littered street. And behind them came tanks. Six, eight . . . a dozen tanks spread wide in a line, gun muzzles pointing ominously forward, steady.

They faced the hordes. Harry Parsons managed a step or two to take up position in line with the others. The sun was hot now. Action Man wished there was time to take a swig at one of the captured water-bottles . . . but there wasn't.

They were almost within range now, running on swiftly, moving steadily through a cloud of dust.

G.I. Joe dropped his gun. Throwing it down at his feet. He looked at Action Man and Action Man began to laugh. Sergeant Jackson began to laugh too, and Harry Parsons sat down. And he laughed.

They were still laughing when the troops stopped at the defence-works and stood looking at them.

"Say, what's with you guys? Whaddya laughing at? Whaddya doing here?"

"Americans!" gurgled G.I. Joe. "Blooming Yanks!"

"Are we happy to see you!" shouted Action Man to the troops standing around them. "By the way, you're not the Seventh Cavalry, are you?"

One of the young soldiers answered. He sounded bewildered. "Seventh Cavalry? Heck, no . . . we're the Forty-second Light Infantry Brigade. Now come on, you guys, get outa there and tell us what's going on."

"Be a pleasure. Give us a hand with our buddy." G.I. Joe and Action Man helped Harry Parsons out on to the road. An officer came racing down the road in a jeep. "Who are you? Whattya doing here?" he wanted to know.

Action Man took time off to take the drink he'd been longing for and then, as briefly as possible, he explained what they were doing.

By mid-day, Harry Parsons was in a field hospital at the beach-head. Sergeant Jackson, his hand bandaged, Action Man and G.I. Joe were in a caravan, facing General Morecombe. He had listened without comment to Action Man's account of the taking of Monte Carrillo.

Now he said: "You men are responsible for the success of the entire advance on this front. While The Hill was there, we were dead ducks. You're going to hear more of this, all of you. Meanwhile, you have my personal thanks . . . and congratulations."

They were about to leave when the General added, "By the way, we found another soldier in Tavati, holed-up in a cellar. He was dead. A mortar shell had landed smack in the doorway. Guess he never knew what hit him. Would he be the guy, Blade, you mentioned?"

Action Man nodded. "I should think so, sir." And he described Blade's appearance.

"That's him." The General's face was grim. "Well, if he'd stayed with you boys, he might have made it. But, after hearing what you've told me . . . maybe he got what was coming to him anyway!"

Outside, Sergeant Jackson shook his head. "You chaps might get a medal out of all this," he said gloomily. "But I know the Army. I know what I'm going to get. I'll get put on a charge for losing a prisoner!"

THE END

HOLD THE BRIDGE

The Bridge at Breve had to be captured from the Germans and kept open. With only a handful of men, Action Man knew that the chances of taking the bridge were remote — but they had to try. And then Action Man met G.I. Joe and the odds swung a little in their favour . . .

SNOW, ICE AND BULLETS

Trapped in Norway by the German invasion, Professor Lindfors, a brilliant scientist, was desperate to escape and work to free his country.

Action Man and G.I. Joe had a top-secret mission — to get the Professor back to England. On reaching Norway, they found that the Germans were one step ahead of them — Professor Lindfors had been taken to the impregnable prison at Castle Richbleau . . .

OPERATION SKY-DROP

The objective: to capture two vital bridges so that the Allies' advance could cross the river.

The plane towing the glider carrying Action Man and G.I. Joe was hit, and the glider had to make a crash-landing on the wrong side of the river. A Panzer division with over 30 tanks was now breathing down their necks and Action Man knew that he must prevent them from advancing on the Allies. There was only one answer — Action Man and G.I. Joe had to put those tanks out of action . . .

TO BE PUBLISHED IN NOVEMBER 1977

Two more ACTION MAN Adventure Stories
by the same author

THE TOUGH WAY OUT

COUNTER-ATTACK

Both at 50p

SOME MORE TITLES PUBLISHED BY
CORGI AND CAROUSEL

THE GOD BENEATH THE SEA
by Leon Garfield and Edward Blishen

At first it was a tiny prick of light — as if the sun had gone too close and caught the immense blue fabric of the sky. It glinted and glittered and presently it was seen to move. Its light cast a great pool of gold in the darkening sea and a curious sound was in the air. A thin wailing that rose at times to a scream . . .

The God Beneath the Sea is a brilliantly original version of the Greek myths — the stories of the flood, of Prometheus, Persephone, Pandora and many others, all set against the vast background of the creation of the gods, their deeds and conflicts, their power over their creature, man . . . And there is the story of Hephaestus, the misshapen artist-god — who, hurled from Olympus by his mother Hera for his ugliness, lives to become — The God Beneath the Sea.

0 552 98012 9   65p.

THE GOLDEN SHADOW
by Leon Garfield and Edward Blishen

Across the continents of the ancient world wandered the Storyteller, enchanting all who heard him with his wondrous tales of the gods. He longed for a glimpse of the all-powerful deities of his stories, and listened eagerly to those who had experienced such encounters. Like the fisherman who had seen Themis, mother of the Fates, and heard her prophesy the birth of a great son to Thetis, goddess of the sea . . .

The Golden Shadow tells how this prophesy came true and follows the Storyteller on his quest for the gods. And interwoven with his journey is the story of Heracles — a magnificent story with all the intense drama and high tragedy that the Greek myths traditionally offer, but in an entirely new and original context.

0 552 99776 5   60p

HERNE THE HUNTER 3: THE BLACK WIDOW
by John McLaglen

Seven men. Seven killers. Five already dead. Struck down by the bloody hand of vengeance. Herne's vengeance . . . Only two remain alive. The Stanwyck twins, Mark and Luke. And they think they're safe behind the thick walls of the lofty mansion called Mount Abora. Protected by an army of hired guns. Protected by the fierce dominant love of their mother. Protected by the thick drifts of snow and ice in the high Sierras. But they weren't reckoning on Herne's cussedness and his bitter determination to finish his quest in blood. Their blood. And they certainly weren't reckoning on his teaming up with the Albino, Whitey Coburn . . .

0 552 10385 3   50p

HERNE THE HUNTER 4: SHADOW OF THE VULTURE
by John McLaglen

Jed Herne had avenged the brutal death of his wife, Louise. He had sought out and killed the seven men responsible. But the killing never stops . . . Now Herne had to travel the length of America, from east to west, in pursuit of Senator Nolan — a man whose money and hatred had financed countless attempts on his life. The man was too dangerous to be allowed to live. However long it took Herne would find him . . . and kill him!

Number Four in a savage new series.

0 552 10431 0   50p

A BRAND NEW SERIES OF ACTION-PACKED AD-
VENTURES WITH THE CREW OF THE STARSHIP
U.S.S. ENTERPRISE . . . Featuring Captain James Kirk,
First Officer Spock, and Dr 'Bones" McCoy . . .

STAR TREK LOG 4
by Alan Dean Foster

After being bombarded with strange radiation, all organic
matter on board the Enterprise starts to shrink — and that
includes the crew; the Enterprise is sent to investigate the
Delta Triangle, a vast and mysterious part of the galaxy
where space ships suddenly disappear: and Cyrano Jones,
interstellar trader and general nuisance, comes aboard the
ship with his cargo of tribbles, innocent little furry creatures
that refuse to stop growing . . .

0 552 10107 9   50p

STAR TREK LOG 5
by Alan Dean Foster

As the Enterprise continues her mission into unknown
realms, Captain Kirk and his crew find themselves
marooned on the weird water-world of Argo, and pursued
by a sea monster; Spock becomes desperately ill with a
disease fatal to Vulcans; and the Skorr go on the war path,
threatening to launch a holy war against the rest of the
civilised galaxy . . .

0 552 10315 2   60p